50p

The Hardy Boys
in
The Mystery of the Disappearing Floor

D1396063

This Armada book belongs to:

_____

_____

_____

The Hardy Boys Mystery Stories

The Mystery of the Disappearing Floor

Franklin W. Dixon

First published in the U.K. in 1971 by
William Collins Sons & Co. Ltd., London and Glasgow.
First published in Armada in 1974 by
Fontana Paperbacks,
14 St. James's Place, London SW1A 1PS.

This impression 1981.

© MCMLXIV Grosset & Dunlap, Inc. All rights reserved
under International and Pan-American copyright conventions.
Published pursuant to agreement with Grosset & Dunlap, Inc.,
New York, N.Y., U.S.A.

© 1971 in Great Britain and the British Commonwealth (except
Canada) by William Collins Sons & Co. Ltd.

Printed in Great Britain by
Love & Malcomson Ltd., Brighton Road,
Redhill, Surrey.

CONDITIONS OF SALE:
This book is sold subject to the condition that
it shall not, by way of trade or otherwise, be lent,
re-sold, hired out or otherwise circulated without
the publisher's prior consent in any form of
binding or cover other than that in which it is
published and without a similar condition
including this condition being imposed on the
subsequent purchaser.

CONTENTS

"Frank! The room has no floor!"

Weird Screams

"HEY, Frank! Isn't that the black car Dad told us to look out for?" exclaimed Joe Hardy.

A sleek foreign sports car with a dented boot had just whizzed past the Hardy boys' convertible as they drove through the downtown section of Bayport.

"Sure looks like it!" Frank speeded up in pursuit.

Dark-haired Frank Hardy, eighteen, and his blond brother Joe, a year younger, had been cruising the streets on an errand for their detective father. The August evening was warm, and the boys had put down the top of their convertible.

A few streets farther on, the sports car stopped at a red light. The Hardys pulled up behind the trim vehicle. In the glow of a nearby street light they were able to scrutinize the car more closely.

"That must be the right one," Frank muttered. "It's not likely there would be two of the same model in Bayport with dented boots."

The lone occupant of the sports car was the man at the wheel. He wore a dark hat. Frank and Joe could see only the back of his head.

"Did Dad give you any details of the case when he phoned?" Joe asked, as the sports car spurted forward on the green signal.

Frank pressed the accelerator and shook his head. "No, he didn't have time—it was just a hurried call from New York." Mr Hardy had said that before leaving Bayport he had spotted a car like the one the boys had just seen. He thought he had recognized the driver as a notorious jewel thief named Noel Strang, and had told his sons to look up the criminal's photograph in Mr Hardy's private criminal file.

The boys' father was formerly an ace detective in the New York Police Department. He had moved to the town of Bayport to open his own agency and soon had become known as one of the ablest private investigators in the country. Frank and Joe had inherited Fenton Hardy's detective abilities and often helped him on his cases.

The boys drove on, staying behind the sports car which now sped into a residential area. The streets here were less well lighted, but the boys were able to keep their quarry in view without tailing it too closely.

"Looks as though he's heading out of town," Joe remarked.

"Did you get the licence number?"

"Yes. I jotted it down at the traffic light."

In a few moments the black sports car shot out of the Bayport area. Soon it disappeared from view around a bend in the road. Frank switched off his headlights, hoping to make the convertible less noticeable. But the driver of the other car seemed wary of pursuit. As the convertible rounded the bend, its driver increased his speed. The distance between the cars was widening.

"He must have spotted us!" Joe said.

"He's sure opening her up," Frank agreed. "That

baby looks powerful! Good thing we tuned up this engine last week."

The convertible's speedometer needle rose as Frank put his foot down. Slowly the gap began to close. They were approaching another bend in the road. Suddenly the sports car's exhaust belched out a thick purplish mass.

"It's a smoke screen!" Joe cried out. "He's using a fogger attachment to the exhaust pipe!" A split second later the boys' eyes began to smart and water.

"Good grief!" Frank exclaimed.

Hastily he switched on their headlights again, but the beams could not pierce the thick pall of acrid smoke that enveloped the road. The convertible was almost at the sharp bend!

Frank slammed on the brakes. Half blinded, he could only guess at the location of the white line. He spun the steering wheel and the car slewed wildly across the road. With a jarring thud it finally came to rest on the far shoulder of the road.

"Jumpin' jiminy!" Joe sat quivering with shock, trying to steady his nerves.

Frank, also shaken, drew a long breath. "Good thing there was no car coming the other way or we'd be junk by now!"

"Can we risk getting back on the road?"

"We'd better not," Frank decided. "I can't see a foot away from us. If there's any traffic coming, we'd be asking for a crash."

Joe agreed and added, "Let's make sure we're clear of the road."

Clutching handkerchiefs over their noses and wiping their streaming eyes, the boys climbed out. In the smoke and darkness, it was impossible to determine their exact position, but Frank checked with his foot and found that they were well off the tarmac. The convertible had landed against a hillside bordering the road.

Frank and Joe chafed at the delay, but there was nothing to do except wait for the smoke to clear. Meanwhile, they clambered up the hillside, coughing and choking, to reach clear air.

"Did you notice the smoke's colour?" Joe gasped. "That was no ordinary smoke screen!"

"Right. Sort of a combination of smoke and tear gas."

After a few minutes the murk had dissipated enough for the boys to return to their car and swing back on to the road.

"Not much chance of finding that man now," Joe said glumly.

"Let's keep our eyes open, anyway. There are houses along here and a few side turnings. We might spot the car parked somewhere."

The Hardys followed the road for several miles but did not see the sports car. Disappointed that they had lost their quarry, Frank and Joe turned round and headed back for Bayport.

Halfway back to town, they saw a light being waved frantically from the roadside. "Wonder if there's been an accident," Frank said.

"I don't see any car," Joe replied. "Must be a hitch-hiker."

Frank slowed to check. The person who was signalling immediately jumped into the glare of their headlights. He was a chunky, round-faced youth about their own age.

"It's a smoke screen!"

"Chet Morton!" Joe exclaimed in surprise.

The stout boy looked excited as he flagged them down. Frank braked to a halt and Joe flung open the car door. "What's wrong, Chet?"

"Joe! Frank! Boy, what a lucky break you two happened along!" Chet was puffing and trembling and looked pale. He was wearing hiking shorts and had a knapsack slung over his shoulders.

"Just see a ghost?" Frank asked as their friend climbed into the back seat.

"I d-d-didn't *see* a ghost—but I sure *heard* one!" Chet replied.

Frank and Joe exchanged puzzled looks. "What do you mean, you 'heard' a ghost?" Frank asked.

"Just what I said. It screamed at me." Chet shuddered. "O-oh, it was horrible!"

"Are you kidding?" Joe put in.

"Do I look as if I'm kidding?"

"No," Frank said. "You look as if you'd been scared out of your wits. How about telling us the whole story?"

Chet explained that he had been on a rock-collecting hike. Late in the afternoon he had stopped to eat a picnic snack and then had dozed off.

"Snack my eye!" Joe chuckled. "You probably stuffed yourself so full you couldn't move, and dreamed about this ghost."

"All right, all right," Chet retorted indignantly. "So I like to eat. Do you want to hear my story or don't you?"

"Go ahead," Frank urged.

"Well, I slept longer than I expected to," Chet went on. "When I woke up, it was dark. I was somewhere over in the hills west of here. I had trouble finding my torch. Then I saw a funny-looking tiled surface."

"Tiled surface?" Joe repeated. "What do you mean by that?"

Chet shrugged. "I don't know what else to call it. It was flat—like a floor, about ten feet square—and inlaid with little coloured tiles. But the funny thing is, there was nothing else around except trees and shrubs."

The coloured tiles, Chet added, formed a curious design resembling a dragon.

"I went over to get a closer look at it," Chet continued, "and wow! Out of nowhere came a horrible bloodcurdling shriek!"

"So you scrammed, I suppose," Frank said, grinning.

"You bet I did! The voice shrieked after me, but I didn't catch what it said." Chet's eyes bulged with fright at the recollection. "I kept running till I hit a muddy lane, and followed that out to this road. I was hiking home, then you guys came along."

"How about taking us back there?" Joe said.

"You think I'm nuts? Honest, if that wasn't a spook, it must have been some bloodthirsty lunatic!"

"Oh, come on!" Frank urged. "Maybe it was just someone playing a trick on you. Let's find out."

Chet was unwilling, but finally gave in. He directed Frank to a side turning which the Hardys had passed about fifty yards back. Frank drove slowly along the lane until Chet said, "Right here! I remember that big oak tree!"

Frank stopped the convertible. The boys took torches and climbed out. They went up a slope which gradually flattened. The area was wooded with spruce and cypress trees, and the ground between them was overgrown with weeds and brush.

"There's Chet's trail," Joe said, shining his light on to some trampled grass. "It leads over that w—"

A hideous scream split the darkness! Then came a weaker scream, followed by a hoarse, croaking voice. "*Th-th-the floor!*" It sounded like the gasp of a dying man!

Chet froze in terror, but Frank and Joe immediately ran towards the sound, playing their beams back and forth amid the undergrowth.

"Over here, Joe!" Frank exclaimed suddenly.

Joe ran to his brother's side and saw a man lying face down on the ground. Frank turned him over gently. The man was big and balding, with thin, sandy-coloured hair. His face looked deathly pale. Frank tried his pulse as Chet came lumbering up.

"Is he d-d-dead?" Chet stammered.

"No, but his pulse is weak," Frank murmured. "His skin feels clammy, too. Looks as if he's suffering from shock."

The Hardys could detect no signs of injury or broken bones.

"What'll we do with him?" Joe asked his brother.

"Better get him to a hospital."

The boys carried the limp figure to their car and laid him on the back seat. Chet sat in the front with the Hardys. Frank swung the convertible round and sped towards Bayport.

As they reached a wooded area on the outskirts of town, their passenger revived and sat up. "Please— stop the car!" he begged weakly.

Frank pulled over. "We were taking you to the hospital," he explained.

"You were unconscious," Joe added. "What happened?"

"I'll—I'll tell you in a moment," the man said. "Right now I feel woozy. I think the motion of the car was making me sick. Would you mind if I get out and walk up and down a bit?"

"No—go ahead," Joe said sympathetically.

Chet leaned back and opened the door. As soon as the man's feet touched the ground, he slammed the door. His face contorted into an ugly expression.

"If you boys know what's good for you, you'll keep your mouths shut about this!" he snarled. "And I'm warning you—don't try to follow me!"

He darted off into the darkness of the surrounding trees!

·2·

Telephone Tip

THE three boys were stunned by the man's unexpected threat and actions.

"Of all the creeps!" Chet spluttered when he found his voice. "How's that for gratitude?"

"I'm going after that guy!" Joe exploded. He yanked open the door and started to jump out, but Frank stopped him.

"Hold it, Joe! You'll never catch him now. Besides, he may be armed."

Joe realized the wisdom of his brother's advice and reluctantly climbed back into the car. The neighbourhood was a bit seedy. It was poorly lighted and had numerous vacant spaces and small factory buildings. The stranger already was out of sight and doubtless could find plenty of hiding places if pursued.

"I'd sure like to know what that fellow was afraid of," Joe muttered as they drove off. "Also, how he came to be lying back there, unconscious."

"So would I," Frank said. "We'd better notify the police."

"Look, fellows, I—uh—I'm pretty tired," Chet said uneasily. "Could you drop me off at home first?"

"What's the matter?" Joe teased. "Afraid the police may hold you as a suspect?"

"I told you I'm bushed!" Chet retorted. "Besides, you Hardys are always getting mixed up with crooks and mysteries. That kind of stuff makes me nervous!"

Frank and Joe grinned in the darkness. It was true that they had worked on a number of exciting cases, some of them a bit hair-raising.

After dropping Chet off at the Morton farm, the Hardys drove to Bayport Police Headquarters. Here they found Chief Collig working late. The husky man smiled broadly as they walked into his office.

"You boys busy on another case?"

"We're helping Dad," Frank explained. "But something else came up." He told Chief Collig about the unconscious man who had later revived in their car and fled after threatening them.

Collig agreed that while the episode was strange, apparently no crime had been committed. He telephoned the fugitive's description to the police radio control room to be flashed to all patrol cars, with orders that the man be picked up for questioning.

Frank told him about the boys' pursuit of the black sports car and the smoke grenade that had forced them off the road.

"Noel Strang, eh?" The chief frowned. "I've heard about him. Slick operator, but he's not on the 'Wanted' list right now. Do you know why your father is after him?"

"No, we don't," Frank said. "Dad just asked us to trail him and try to get a line on what he's up to."

"We got the licence number," Joe added. "But we'd like to know if the man we were following was Strang. We didn't get a good look at him."

Collig jotted down the number. "I'll check it with the

Motor Vehicle Bureau. I appreciate your looking in."

The boys went outside to their convertible. As Frank felt in his pocket for the car keys, his expression changed to one of annoyance. "I've lost my penknife, Joe. Wonder if it dropped out back there when I was bending over that fellow?"

"Could be," Joe said. "We can search for it tomorrow. I want to take a look at that tiled square Chet told us about."

"Same here!"

Frank took the wheel and drove off through the late evening traffic. Suddenly a red light flashed on their dashboard short-wave radio. Joe picked up the microphone.

"Joe Hardy here."

"Good evening, son." Fenton Hardy's voice came over the speaker.

"Dad! When did you get home?"

"Just arrived. Where are you fellows now?"

"We're in town. In fact, we're headed for home."

"Good. This case I'm working on looks pretty tough and I may need your help. I'll have to leave again first thing in the morning, so I'd like to give you the details this evening."

"We'll be there pronto, Dad!"

A short time later the convertible pulled into the driveway of the Hardys' large, pleasant house on a tree-shaded street. The boys jumped out of the car and hurried inside.

Fenton Hardy, a tall, rugged-looking man, was in the dining room having a cup of coffee. Seated at the table with him were Mrs Hardy and the boys' Aunt Gertrude, his unmarried sister.

The detective greeted Frank and Joe with a warm smile. "Sit down, boys, and I'll tell you what this case is all about."

Mr Hardy explained that he had been asked by a group of insurance underwriters to investigate a series of jewel thefts. The latest had occurred in New York the day before.

"We heard a news flash on that, Dad!" Joe exclaimed.

"Undoubtedly all the thefts have been pulled by the same gang," the detective went on. "And there's an odd feature. On every job, the guards or other persons involved seem to have lost their memory for a short period of time while the robbery was taking place."

"You mean they passed out?" Frank asked.

Fenton Hardy shrugged. "None of them *recalls* passing out. But they all report a sensation of coming to, or snapping out of a deep sleep, as if they had lapsed into unconsciousness without realizing it."

Gertrude Hardy, a tall, angular woman, pursed her lips and frowned shrewdly. "If you ask me, they were gassed," she declared. "Some kind of nerve gas, probably—squirted at the victims through a blowpipe."

Frank and Joe tried hard not to grin. Their aunt had definite opinions and never hesitated to express them.

"They may have been gassed," Mr Hardy agreed. "But if so, it's strange that police experts were unable to discover any traces in the atmosphere afterwards."

"Maybe the crooks sucked it all back into their blowpipes," Joe said mischievously.

Aunt Gertrude gave him a withering look. "Making fun of me, are you? Well, maybe you have a better theory, young man!"

Laura Hardy, a slim and pretty woman, exchanged a fleeting smile with her husband. Both knew that Aunt Gertrude loved to talk about detective cases with her brother and the boys, even though she pretended to disapprove of such dangerous work.

"Matter of fact, we got gassed ourselves tonight," Frank put in quietly. He told them about their chase of the black sports car, but glossed over the part about skidding across the road.

"*Hmm.*" Fenton Hardy knit his brows. "Do you think the driver could have recognized you—maybe from seeing your picture in the paper?"

Frank shook his head. "I doubt it, although he may have glimpsed us in his rear-view mirror when we passed a street light. I think that when he spotted our car tailing him, he used the smoke screen to shake us off."

"Why, that man's a menace!" Aunt Gertrude blurted out indignantly. "Why didn't you radio the police at once? Mark my words, you'll—"

The ringing of the telephone interrupted Aunt Gertrude's prediction. Joe jumped up to answer it.

"Let me speak to Fenton Hardy," said a curt, muffled voice.

"Who's calling, please?" Joe asked.

"None of your business! Just tell him to get on the phone if he wants to learn something important!"

Fenton Hardy strode quickly to Joe's side and took the receiver. "All right, I'm listening."

"Another jewel theft has been planned. It's going to be pulled aboard a yacht named the *Wanda.* She's due in at East Hampton, Long Island, late tonight or early tomorrow morning. Got that?"

"I have it," the detective replied. "But who is this speaking?"

"A friend. And don't bother trying to trace the call!"

There was a click at the other end of the line. Mr Hardy hung up thoughtfully and told the boys what the informer had said.

"I'd better follow up that tip-off," he added. "I'll drive down to East Hampton."

"Are you sure that's wise, Dad?" Frank asked worriedly. "The call may be a trick."

"It's a chance I'll have to take, son."

Mr Hardy telephoned Suffolk County Police Head-quarters on Long Island to report the tip. Before leaving the house, he suggested that the boys study the photo of Strang in his file, and also the typewritten data on the reverse side of it.

"Mind you, we have nothing on him," the detective said. "But I think he's one of the few jewel thieves in the country capable of master-minding a series of robberies like the ones I'm investigating."

"Do you want the police to take him in for questioning?" Joe asked.

"No, that would only put him on guard. But I *would* like to know what he's doing in Bayport!"

"We'll keep an eye open for him," Frank promised.

Mr Hardy then placed a long-distance call to his top-flight operative, Sam Radley. Sam had flown to Florida with a charter pilot named Jack Wayne to wind up another case. Fenton Hardy instructed Sam to join him at East Hampton the following day.

Next morning, Frank and Joe ate a hearty breakfast of bacon, eggs, and home-made muffins, then started off in their convertible to pick up Chet Morton. After some grumbling, the stout boy agreed to help them search for the curious tiled square he had seen the night before. The three boys drove to the lane near the big oak tree.

"I don't know why I let you two talk me into this," Chet complained as they started up the slope. "I can't seem to stay out of danger when you're around."

Joe laughed. "Stop griping. You don't expect to hear any spooks in broad daylight, do you?"

When they reached level ground, Frank remarked, "Say, I see a house over there!"

Joe and Chet looked in the direction he was pointing. A large, weather-beaten mansion was visible through the trees some distance away.

"Didn't notice any lights over that way last night," Joe said, "Wonder if anyone lives there."

"Maybe not," Frank said. "Looks pretty run down."

For half an hour the boys searched among the tall weeds and overgrown shrubbery. They failed to sight the tiled surface Chet had described, or to find Frank's knife.

"Sure you weren't just seeing things last night?" Frank asked Chet.

Joe chuckled. "Maybe just hearing things, too?"

Before Chet could reply, a voice barked out, "Stand right where you are! Now turn round, all three of you!"

The boys whirled in surprise. A tall, hawk-faced man with a thin, prominent nose was standing among the trees watching them. He had one hand in his jacket pocket, as if concealing a gun.

Frank and Joe gasped. The man looked like the photograph of Noel Strang in their father's files!

·3·

The Purple Stone

"DON'T stand there gaping!" the man snarled. "What are you kids looking for?"

Chet gulped. "W-well—uh—you see, l-last night—"

"I lost my penknife," Frank spoke up. "We were trying to find it."

"Your penknife, eh?" The man scowled at the boys suspiciously. "You had no business nosing around here last night or anytime. This is private property. Now clear out!"

Chet, overcome with jitters, hastily started walking back to the car. Frank and Joe did not budge, and continued to stare at the man.

"You heard me!" he said in a loud, belligerent voice. "Beat it! And don't come back!"

He took a few steps towards the Hardys and crooked his arm as if he were about to jerk his gun hand out of his pocket. Without a word, the brothers turned and followed Chet.

"That *is* Noel Strang!" Joe whispered. "Think we should call his bluff?"

Frank shook his head. "Not now. Remember what Dad said."

"He may not own this property," Joe argued. "If he does, maybe we can find out what he's doing here."

"I intend to," Frank said. "But let's try to do it undercover, without making him suspicious."

Chet had already climbed into the car. He was sitting stiffly in the back seat—still pale and nervous, but whistling off-key and trying to look casual.

Frank slid behind the wheel and Joe got in beside him. As they glanced back up the slope, the boys could see Strang watching them intently.

"Oh—oh," Joe muttered. "I just thought of something!"

"Like what?" Frank asked.

"If he's the one who used that smoke screen last night, he may recognize our convertible."

"Smoke screen!" Chet gasped. In the rear-view mirror, Frank could see that the fat boy's eyes were bulging with fear. "You mean that guy's a gangster?"

"Not exactly," Joe said, as Frank turned the car round. "Just a notorious jewel thief named Noel Strang."

Chet groaned as the Hardys told him the details. "Oh, this is great! I don't want to get mixed up in another one of your cases! You'd better take me home."

The Hardys grinned. "Chet, you know you eat up excitement as well as food," Frank said.

"It helps to keep your weight trimmed down," Joe suggested.

"Listen! I'll probably lose ten pounds just worrying about this thief," Chet retorted. "Strang may even send his men after us!"

Joe chuckled. "Just threaten to sit on 'em—that'll be enough of a scare."

Frank suddenly looked troubled. "Now *I* just thought of something, Joe."

"Bad?" Joe glanced at his brother.

"Not good. That knife has my name engraved on it. If Strang finds the knife, he may connect us with Fenton Hardy."

Joe gave a low whistle. "Let's hope he *doesn't* find it!"

A short time later Frank swung up the gravelled driveway leading to the Mortons' farmhouse. Chet's pretty, dark-haired sister Iola was seated on the front porch with her blonde, brown-eyed friend Callie Shaw.

Iola bounced up from the porch swing as the boys stepped from the car. "Hi!" she exclaimed. "Wait'll you see the surprise Callie and I have to show you!" The girls' eyes sparkled with excitement.

Joe grinned at Iola, whom he considered very attractive. "Sounds pretty important."

"Aw, it's probably some new gee-gaws for their charm bracelets," Chet scoffed.

"Like fun!" Iola retorted. "It'll make you turn green with envy—I mean purple!"

As the boys followed the two girls into the house, Callie explained that she and Iola had been rock hunting the day before. With a giggle, she also whispered to Frank that Chet and Iola were keen rivals at rock hunting.

In the dining room, Iola went straight to the old-fashioned punch bowl on the sideboard and took out a stone about the size of a grape. It was pale violet and roughly crystalline in form.

"Feast your eyes!" she said, waving the stone under Chet's nose.

"Well, hold it still so I can see it." The chubby youth stared in grudging admiration.

"It's beautiful," Frank said. "Is that an amethyst?"

Iola bobbed her head proudly. "A real one!"

"We took it to Filmer's Gemstone Shop this morning to make sure," Callie added. "Mr Filmer identified it for us."

Chet's eyes nearly popped out in awe. "Wow! A real jewel!" he gasped. "Where'd you find it?"

Iola and Callie blushed with embarrassment. "We don't remember," Iola confessed.

"You don't remember?" Chet echoed. "How stupid can you get! Why, there might be a whole lode of amethysts around the spot!"

"But we picked up oodles of stones in several places," Callie explained. "The light wasn't good in the late afternoon and we didn't realize that this one might be valuable."

"We're not even sure which one of us found it," Iola put in. "We didn't get excited until we sorted the stones this morning."

Chet was about to make a wisecrack when Joe happened to glance out the window.

"Hey!" he yelled. "Your barn's on fire!"

The others stared and gasped. Black smoke was billowing out through the open barn door!

"Good grief!" Chet shouted. "And Dad's over at the vet's this morning! Quick! Get some fire extinguishers and buckets of water!"

The five teenagers dashed outside, followed by Mrs Morton, who had hurried upstairs from the cellar when she heard their cries.

There was no sign of open flames from the barn, so Frank and Chet plunged inside to get the pair of fire extinguishers hanging on the wall. Joe and the girls, meanwhile, formed a bucket brigade from the pump.

"Oh, my goodness!" Mrs Morton cried distractedly as she hovered outside the barn. "Shall I call the fire station?"

"Don't bother, Mom!" Chet shouted back. "This looks like a false alarm!"

Soon the smoke began to clear and the two boys emerged, grimy from the thick fumes. "A bucket of oil was burning," Frank explained, coughing.

"Sure beats me how it started," Chet added. "I wouldn't think heavy tractor oil could ignite by spontaneous combustion."

Relieved, they all trooped back to the house. Mrs Morton provided soap and towels for Chet and Frank to wash in the kitchen. Joe and the girls returned to the dining room.

Iola went to pick up the amethyst but could not find it. "Callie, did you take our jewel outside with you?" she asked.

"No, you left it on the table, didn't you?"

"I thought I did." Iola hastily checked the punch bowl, then turned an anxious face to the others. "It's not here!"

A frantic search followed, with Joe scrabbling on the floor and the girls going through every drawer and compartment of the sideboard. The amethyst was gone! Frank and Chet heard the news as they came into the dining room.

"Oh, fine!" Chet groaned. "First a fire, and now you girls lose the only valuable stone we've ever found!"

Frank and Joe looked at each other with the same thought in mind.

"I'll bet that fire was a trick to get us out of the house!" Joe exclaimed.

"You mean the stone was *stolen?*" Iola gasped.

"I'm afraid so," Frank said. "By the same person who set fire to that bucket of oil."

Callie's eyes glowed with a sudden recollection. "I heard a car start up down the road just as we came back to the house!" she said. "I'll bet that was the thief getting away!"

Chet plumped himself down in a chair. "Boy, this is turning out to be quite a day." He grunted, then brightened. "Suppose we may as well have lunch."

Frank telephoned a report of the theft to the police and then called home to notify his mother that he and Joe would be lunching at the Mortons'.

Aunt Gertrude took the message. "By the way," she said, "Tony Prito has called twice, trying to get hold of you and Joe. Wouldn't tell me what he wanted, but he did say it was urgent."

"Where can I call him?" Frank asked. "At his dad's office?"

"*Mmm*—no, I believe he said he was phoning from the boat dock."

"Okay, Aunty. Thanks."

Frank and Joe apologized to Mrs Morton for hurrying through the hearty lunch she served them. As soon as they had finished, the brothers excused themselves to go and find Tony Prito.

Tony, a dark-haired, good-looking boy, was a close chum of the Hardys and they often went out on Barmet Bay with him in his motor-boat, the *Napoli*. Frank and Joe drove quickly to the boat harbour but could not see Tony anywhere.

"I'll bet he's out in the *Napoli*," Joe said, staring out across the harbour.

"Probably so." Frank glanced up at the sunny sky and then at the gentle white-capped blue waters of the bay. "Let's get the *Sleuth*, Joe, and try to find him."

"Suits me."

The Hardys hurried off to the boathouse where they kept their own motor boat.

At that moment Tony was just driving up to the Mortons' house in his father's pick-up truck.

"Hi, Chet! Have you seen Frank and Joe today?" he called to the stout youth, who had come out to the porch.

"Sure. They had lunch here. Left about fifteen minutes ago, heading for the harbour to find you."

Tony suddenly went pale. "Oh no! I hope they don't go out in the *Sleuth!*"

"Why not?" Chet asked, puzzled.

"Hop in and I'll tell you. We'd better get there fast!"

Chet hardly had time to get into the cab before Tony threw the truck into reverse. As he swung the vehicle round and sped off down the road, he explained, "I saw two tough-looking guys sneak out of Frank and Joe's boathouse. Somehow I have a hunch those men were up to no good!"

"Did you recognize them?" Chet asked, wide-eyed.

"No, but I'm afraid those men may have sabotaged it!"

"Didn't you warn Mrs Hardy and Aunt Gertrude?"

"Guess I should have," Tony said ruefully. "But I didn't want to alarm them."

As the truck pulled up on the quay, Chet exclaimed and pointed towards the water. "There they go now!"

The *Sleuth*, with two figures aboard, was putt-putting out across the bay.

"We're too late," Tony groaned.

The boys leaped out of the truck and began shouting and waving frantically to their friends. But the Hardys' boat was too far out for the brothers to hear the cries.

Suddenly a loud explosion shook the *Sleuth!*

·4·

The Jigsaw Face

THE force of the blast jerked the bow of the *Sleuth* up out of the water! Both its occupants were hurled overboard and the boat itself overturned. Smoke billowed from the scene.

"Come on!" Tony cried to Chet. "We must get out there and pick them up!"

"Where's the *Napoli?*" Chet puffed as they ran along the quay.

"I left it tied up at the North Dock."

People were already gathering excitedly along the waterfront. The two boys reached the North Dock and leaped into the motor boat. Chet cast off and Tony gunned the outboard into life. In a moment they were speeding out on the bay.

Chet, who was seated in the bow, shouted in relief, "Looks as if Frank and Joe are okay!"

The Hardys had been struggling in the water, but could now be seen clinging to their overturned craft. The *Napoli* came alongside.

"Well, this is what I call service!" Joe said as he and Frank were hauled aboard.

Tony explained, "We came to give you a warning."

"Tony, *we* came out here looking for *you*," Joe replied. "Your boat wasn't in the basin."

"No, I took it out this morning and tied up at the North Dock when I came back."

"What did you mean about warning us?" Frank put in.

Tony hastily told about seeing two men sneak out of the boathouse. Just as he finished, a Coast Guard rescue launch reached the scene. Other boats were approaching also.

"Everybody okay?" the chief petty officer called out from the Coast Guard launch.

"They're okay but very wet," Chet replied.

"What happened?" the officer asked.

"Some kind of explosion in the forward compartment," Frank told him. "We suspect sabotage."

The chief ordered his coxs'n to maneouvre the launch closer to the overturned craft. A hole had been blown in the hull near the bow, but the boat's special flotation apparatus in the forward space had kept it from sinking.

"Can your friends tow the boat to a repair dock all right?" the chief asked the Hardys.

"We can manage, if someone will give us a hand," Tony spoke up.

"I'll help you, lads!" called a man from a nearby motor cruiser.

"In that case, I'd like you fellows to come back to the Coast Guard station with me and make a report," the officer told Frank and Joe.

The Hardys transferred to the Coast Guard launch, which immediately sped off to its base. Meanwhile, Tony and Chet tackled the job of putting a towline on to the *Sleuth*, with the help of the man in the motor cruiser.

At the Coast Guard station Frank and Joe told their

story to a lieutenant named Anson. "You're Fenton Hardy's sons, aren't you?" he asked.

"Yes, sir," Joe answered.

"Is this sabotage connected with one of his cases?"

Frank hesitated. "We think so, sir, but we don't know yet."

Lieutenant Anson asked, "Any theories?"

"Someone was trying to kill us, or at least scare us off our investigation," Frank said. "My guess is that the bomb was detonated chemically in some way by the salt water. But I have a hunch it went off too soon—the saboteurs hoped we'd be farther out in the bay."

"Right," Joe agreed. "I'll bet the blast was supposed to swamp the boat fast, drown us, and send all our evidence against them to the bottom. But luckily for us, the boat overturned and stayed afloat, giving us something to cling to—"

Lieutenant Anson took down their statements, then said, "For the record, I'll say you're carrying out your own investigation. But please keep us informed."

He had a man drive the boys back to their car. Frank and Joe went home, where Aunt Gertrude greeted them with clucks of disapproval.

"Well, I never! It's a good thing your mother has gone to the library board meeting!" Miss Hardy ordered the boys to take off their soaked shoes to avoid dirtying the carpet, then went on anxiously, "What happened? Did that crook you're after make you walk the plank?"

Frank chuckled and gave her a damp hug, which Miss Hardy tried to fend off. "Slight accident, Aunty—a ducking we didn't expect."

The boys had just changed into dry clothes when

the telephone rang. Joe answered. The caller was Chief Collig.

"Got a report from the Motor Vehicle Bureau on that sports car licence number," he said. "It's registered in the name of Aden Darrow."

"Never heard of him," Joe replied.

"Nothing on him in our files, either."

"What about the address?"

"A street number in Eastern City," Collig said. "I checked with the police there but they couldn't help. The whole street's been demolished for a motorway."

"Dead-end clue. Well, thanks a lot, Chief."

A short time later Tony Prito and Chet arrived. They reported that the *Sleuth* had been safely towed to the repair dock. Frank telephoned to determine the cost of repairing the boat, then the boys gathered to discuss the day's events. Frank and Joe quickly told Tony about the case.

"You think the men who planted the bomb were working for Strang?" Tony asked.

"Could be," Frank said. "Especially if he found my knife and learned our name."

"I'll bet he recognized us last night!" Joe put in.

"How about that sneak who took Iola and Callie's amethyst?" Chet asked. "Maybe Strang did that too. You said he's a jewel thief."

Frank frowned. "That's true. But he's a big-time operator. I doubt if the amethyst's worth enough to tempt him."

"Anyhow, Strang's definitely got business in this area," Joe said. "Do you think he could be hiding out at that old house—the one we saw him near this morning?"

"Could be," Frank said.

Tony asked where the place was located. When Joe told him, Miss Hardy exclaimed, "Why, that's the old Perth mansion!"

"Do you know who lives there?" Frank asked.

"No one, so far as I've heard," she replied. "Hasn't been occupied for years. The place had what you might call a sinister reputation."

"Why is that?" Joe inquired.

"Seems someone died there under mysterious circumstances. Don't recollect just who. But there was talk about the place being haunted."

"Haunted?" Chet swallowed and turned pale.

Miss Hardy sniffed. "All stuff and nonsense. Some folks will believe anything. That was years ago—even before you boys were born."

"Tell us some more, Aunty," Frank urged.

Gertrude Hardy settled into her favourite chair. "Well, the house originally belonged to a man named Jerome Perth. Not a nice person at all, from what folks used to say."

"Who was he?" Frank asked.

"Some sort of big business tycoon—but a shady operator. People accused him of all sort of things—stock swindles, patent infringements. I don't know what all. But I suppose no one ever pinned anything on him."

"Must have been pretty clever," Tony remarked.

"Oh, he was," Miss Hardy agreed. "And he made a lot of enemies—in fact, some of the people he'd cheated even tried to kill him. Finally he retired to that mansion he built and lived there in fear of his life."

"So his swindles didn't bring him any happiness," Joe remarked.

"No, indeed. I recall hearing he had his study on the ground floor fitted up with a bed and hardly ever stirred out of that one room."

"But you still don't remember who died there under mysterious circumstances?" Joe said.

Aunt Gertrude shook her head. "Some relative, I think. But I don't recall the details."

Frank, meanwhile, had a sudden hunch. He telephoned Iola Morton to ask if anyone else had been in the gemstone shop when the girls showed the proprietor their amethyst.

"Why, yes, there was," Iola replied. "Another customer came in right after we did. I remember he asked us where we had found our stone." Suddenly Iola gasped. "Oh! You mean maybe *he* was the one who stole our amethyst?"

"Could be," Frank said. "He might have shadowed you back to your house. Is Callie still there with you?"

"Yes. Want to talk to her?"

"We'll come out."

Five minutes later Frank, Joe, and Chet were on their way to the farm in the Hardys' convertible. Tony had to go back to work at his father's construction company.

When the boys arrived at the Mortons' house, Frank carried in his father's facial identification kit. Besides an illuminated viewing screen, the kit contained strips of film showing hundreds of different hairlines, eyes, ears, noses, chins, spectacles, and hats.

Iola and Callie were fascinated as the Hardys began asking them to describe and identify the features of the stranger at the gem shop.

"It's like putting together a jigsaw puzzle!" Callie exclaimed.

Bit by bit, the film strips showing the man's features were laid together over the viewing screen until a whole face had been assembled.

"For Pete's sake!" Joe exclaimed. He and Frank stared at each other. "That's the guy we picked up unconscious last night!"

Chet peered over their shoulders, open-mouthed with surprise. "It is for a fact!"

"Joe," Frank said, "suppose you take that face to the gem shop and ask Mr Filmer if he knows the man."

"Okay. How about you?"

"I want to go to the *Bayport Times* office and see if I can dig up any stories on the Perth mansion from their back files."

Joe dropped his brother off at the newspaper office and a few minutes later pulled up in front of Filmer's Gemstone Shop. He carried the kit inside and spoke to the proprietor.

Mr Filmer, a skinny man with thick bifocal spectacles, seemed oddly nervous. "I—uh—r-really don't recall anyone else being in the shop when Iola and Callie were here," he stammered.

"Please try to remember," Joe begged.

"I'm afraid I can't."

"All right. At least let me show you a picture of the man's face and see if you—" Suddenly Joe broke off. The door to the back room was ajar and he had just seen it move slightly.

Someone was eavesdropping behind the door!

"So that's why Filmer won't help me!" Joe thought. "I'll bet he's afraid of the person hiding back there!"

The young detective wondered what to do. If he asked Mr Filmer's permission to look into the back room, it would forewarn the eavesdropper. But if he acted on impulse—Joe darted behind the counter and yanked open the door.

A tall, sandy-haired man, who looked like the one in the picture, streaked across the back room towards a window! Joe rushed forward and lunged at him. The stranger grabbed a stool and hurled it at Joe.

The stool struck Joe on the temple and he sank to the floor unconscious!

· 5 ·

Spook Hound

As Joe regained consciousness, he felt something cold and damp on his forehead. He was propped in a corner of the gem shop's back room and Mr Filmer was bending over him, applying a wet towel to the bruise.

"Feel all right?" Mr Filmer asked anxiously.

"I—I think so, except for a sore head."

"Dear me! You have quite a lump there!"

"Never mind that." Joe struggled to his feet. "What about that chap who slugged me with a stool?"

Mr Filmer pointed helplessly to an open window. "He got away and ran off down the alley."

"I suppose he's the one who was here when Iola and Callie brought in their amethyst?" Joe said, repressing an angry comment.

Mr Filmer reddened. "I'm terribly sorry I had to lie to you. He was hiding back there all the time, listening. I was too frightened to talk."

"Well, he's not here now—so who is he?"

"I really don't know," Mr Filmer said, looking bewildered. "He often drops into the shop to talk to the local rock hunters, and always seems especially interested in amethysts. That's about all I can tell you."

"When did he get here?" Joe asked.

"Just a few minutes before you did. He asked me if

41

anyone had been inquiring about him. When I said No, he warned me to keep my mouth shut or else he'd have me beaten up. Then he saw you coming and ducked into the back room."

"If he ever shows up again," Joe said, "will you try to notify the police right away?"

"I certainly will!" Mr Filmer nodded vigorously, eager to make amends.

Joe thought of trying to find some fingerprints, but he remembered that the man had been wearing gloves. Before leaving, Joe telephoned a report of the incident to Chief Collig.

When Joe reached home, his mother insisted upon applying a soothing dressing to his swollen temple. Aunt Gertrude hovered close by, supervising the treatment and muttering darkly about the dangers of detective work. Joe merely grinned at her sharp comments.

Soon afterwards, Frank arrived home. He took one look at Joe, who was curled in an easy chair watching TV, then let out a whistle.

"Where'd you get that decoration?"

"I connected with a stool," Joe said wryly. He told Frank what had happened at the gem shop and added, "I still can't figure how that man knew we'd go there to check on him."

"Probably followed the same line of reasoning we did," Frank replied. "The girls picked up the amethyst yesterday—so the shop is the only place where an outsider could have learned about their find. Besides, he had quizzed Iola and Callie about the stone, and you say Filmer knew of his interest in amethysts."

"In other words, he guessed we might put two and

two together. Rather than take any chances, he decided to bulldoze Filmer into silence."

Frank nodded, and Joe added, "Now how about telling me what *you* found out."

"I got the full story," Frank said eagerly. "The person who died at the Perth mansion under mysterious circumstances was Old Man Perth's nephew. Must have been quite sensational. The *Times* had a flock of old write-ups on it."

Joe's eyes brightened with interest. "What happened?"

"Well, the nephew—Clarence Perth—moved into the mansion after Jerome Perth passed away from a heart attack. He took over the old man's bedroom-study. But he lived only a few days to enjoy his inheritance."

"How come?"

"One night, long after midnight, the servants heard him scream in terror," Frank continued. "They broke into the room and found him lying on the floor with his skull fractured. And get this—just before he died, the nephew muttered something which sounded like '*the floor*'!"

Joe gave a whistle. "Wow! When Chet hears that, he'll be positive it was a ghost that screamed at us last night."

"There's more," Frank went on. "Both the door and the windows of the room had been locked from the inside and none of them broken—so there was no way a killer could have entered the room or escaped."

"How about trap doors or trick wall panels?"

Frank shrugged. "The stories said the police looked for secret exits but didn't find any. Of course, criminal-detection methods then weren't what they are today."

"What about the ghost angle?" Joe queried.

"There are several follow-up news items. They said that a number of persons had reported seeing a ghostly figure prowling about the Perth estate."

"Humph! No doubt there'll always be gullible simpletons!" said a peppery voice. Aunt Gertrude planted herself in an easy chair and began darning socks. "Don't mind me." She sniffed. "Just go right on with your wild talk."

Frank and Joe exchanged grins, knowing their aunt was eager to hear more. She looked gratified when Frank repeated the information he had gleaned from the *Bayport Times*.

"Yes, I remember now about Perth's nephew," Miss Hardy said reminiscently. "Poor fellow! Almost seemed as if Fate had marked him out to pay for his uncle's misdeeds."

At dinner Frank and Joe were silent and thoughtful. Neither believed that the weird screams they had heard near the Perth mansion could have been made by the nephew's ghost. Nevertheless, it was an eerie notion!

"I'd like to go back to that mansion," Joe said as the family finished dessert. "I have a hunch we'll find some answers there—about the ghost and Strang too."

Frank agreed. "We'll go as soon as it's dark."

Two hours later the brothers climbed into their convertible and headed towards the outskirts of Bayport. Their tyres hummed in the still, moonlit night air and wispy clouds covered the sky. When they turned on to the lane, Frank switched off their headlights and soon afterwards pulled in close to a screen of shrubbery.

"Better take our torches," Joe murmured.

The savage dog was ready to spring!

The boys got out and headed up the slope. In the distance they could see a few gleams of light from the house.

"Someone's in the haunted house!" Joe remarked. "Maybe Strang. We'd better watch our step!"

The Hardys threaded their way among the trees and underbrush. Suddenly a ferocious snarl made them whirl to the left.

A huge, savage-looking hound stood facing them, its eyes glowing in the dark like coals of fire! Again it snarled, and seemed about to spring at the two intruders!

"Come on! Don't argue with it!" Frank muttered. He started to back away hastily, but Joe clutched his arm.

"Wait, Frank! That thing's not alive—it's just a mechanical dummy!"

Incredulous, Frank looked again. Then he realized that Joe was right. "Well, I'll be a mouldy dog biscuit!" he gasped. "That hound sure looks real enough to bite your head off!"

"We must have crossed an invisible beam that made it light up and snarl," Joe surmised. He reached out a hand to touch the device, as if to reassure himself that the "dog" was not flesh and blood.

"Hold it, Joe!" Frank jerked his brother's hand away. "That thing looks like metal—it may be electrically charged."

Stripping off his belt, Frank held the leather end and swung the buckle lightly against the mechanical hound. A hissing blue-white spark illuminated the darkness as metal touched metal!

"Wow!" Joe gasped. "That really would have given me a jolt! Say, Frank, do you suppose the guy we found here could have been shocked unconscious by some electrified gadget?"

"Sounds like a good guess. And that gives us another reason for watching our step."

More cautiously than ever, the Hardys approached the old mansion. The house, covered with fading planks, was fronted by a low veranda and topped off with turrets and decaying latticework. Ragged clumps of shrubbery grew close to the walls.

"Let's try those lighted windows on the ground floor," Frank suggested.

The boys crept close enough to peer inside. Bookshelves, a desk, chairs, a bureau, and a bed lined the walls of the room.

"This must have been Jerome Perth's bedroom-study," Joe whispered.

He brought his face up closer to the pane for a better view, then gave a cry of astonishment. "Frank, look! *The room has no floor!*"

·6·

Symbol in Brass

FOR a moment Frank thought his brother must be joking. Then he, too, put his face to the window-pane. *Beneath the room's furniture he could see only gaping darkness!*

"This is crazy!" Frank muttered. "That furniture can't just stand in mid-air!"

"If only we could see better," Joe said, flattening his nose against the glass in an effort to peer downwards. Suddenly Frank gave a warning hiss and yanked Joe into a crouching position.

"What's wrong?" Joe whispered.

Frank pointed off beyond the rear of the house. In the distance a tiny light could be seen moving among the trees. The boys shrank back into the shadows of the shrubbery.

As they waited, Joe's eyes fell on what looked like an old coin. It was lying on the ground in the patch of light outside the window. Joe reached out and pocketed it.

Meanwhile, the oncoming beam was zigzagging slowly about the grounds. Minutes went by. A night breeze sighed eerily among the spruce and cypress trees. Bit by bit, the light moved closer to the boys' hiding place.

Frank strained his eyes in the darkness. Suddenly

his scalp prickled. "Joe!" he gasped. "Do you see what I do?"

"I sure do!" Joe gulped.

The light was carried by a ghostly white-robed figure!
But common sense told the boys the figure must be human.

"This is our chance to lay that spook story to rest once and for all," Frank whispered.

Joe glanced at his brother. "You mean we rush the ghost?"

"Right—but not yet. Wait till I give the word."

The white figure flitted along, pausing every so often amidst the tall undergrowth. For a time it seemed to be approaching the house. Then the light moved off in another direction.

Frank put his mouth close to Joe's ear. "Let's sneak up and take Mr Spook by surprise now!"

Silent as shadows, the Hardys darted out from the shrubbery. Moving with swift steps, they closed in towards the phantom figure. But Joe, over-eager, caught his foot in a tangle of undergrowth and thudded to the ground.

The "ghost" whirled, evidently startled by the noise. The flashlight it was carrying raked the two boys, then winked out abruptly. An instant later the figure had slipped away into the darkness!

Frank halted only long enough to make sure his brother was unhurt, then raced in pursuit. Joe scrambled to his feet.

By now the white-robed figure was nowhere to be seen. Then Joe suddenly glimpsed something pale among the trees. Was the spook trying to evade them by doubling back towards the house? Joe sprinted to intercept it.

He saw the phantom figure pass between two trees. Instantly the faint ringing of an alarm bell could be heard from inside the mansion!

"There must be another electronic-eye beam between those trees!" Joe realized.

Floodlights blazed on around the house. The front door burst open and three men dashed outside. The ghost, meanwhile, had veered to the left and was disappearing into the darkness again—this time towards the road, but away from the Hardys' car.

Joe halted, uncertain what to do next. If he continued the pursuit, he would risk being cut off by the men from the house before he could get back to the convertible.

"For all I know, they may be the ones who blew up our boat!" he said to himself.

As the men came closer, Joe made a fast decision and darted off among the trees. A moment later he was startled by a rustle of shrubbery close by. A shadowy figure was running alongside him! "You okay, Joe?"

"Yes. But wow! Don't give me heart failure like that!"

The sounds of pursuit grew fainter and presently the two boys reached sloping ground and headed towards their car.

Both boys hopped into the convertible. Frank turned the starter and the engine came alive with a roar. Spinning the wheel, he sent the car zooming down the lane. "Talk about fast getaways—!" Joe panted as they reached the highway.

"Did you get a look at those men from the house?" Frank asked.

"Not too good a look, but I think one of them may have been Noel Strang."

As the brothers came in the kitchen door of the Hardy home, they heard a loud buzz from the basement.

"The short-wave radio signal!" Frank exclaimed. He and Joe hurried downstairs and switched on the powerful set which the Hardys used for secret communications.

"Fenton H. calling Bayport. Come in, please." The last word swelled to stronger volume as Joe tuned the receiver.

"Bayport to Fenton," Frank said. "We read you loud and clear!"

"Good! I hoped I'd catch you boys in."

"How'd that telephone tip work out?" Frank inquired eagerly.

"It hasn't so far," Mr Hardy reported. "The *Wanda* didn't arrive until six this evening. Its passengers are all wealthy people, and there's a fair amount of jewellery aboard. But as yet we haven't turned up a single clue that might indicate a robbery is planned."

"Do you think the tip was phoney?"

"Too early to tell yet. The police have a dragnet out but they haven't spotted any likely suspects. Of course it's possible the jewel thieves called off the job for some reason."

"Dad, it's also possible the gang wants you stymied there in East Hampton while they prepare to pull a job somewhere else," Frank pointed out.

"That's what I'm afraid of," Mr Hardy agreed. "Meanwhile, Sam and I can't do much. What's the picture there in Bayport?"

Frank rapidly briefed his father on the day's developments. Mr Hardy was stunned to hear about the bombing of the *Sleuth* and the attack on Joe at Filmer's Gemstone Shop. Also, he was intrigued by the Motor Vehicle Bureau's report.

"I'm sure I've heard that name, Aden Darrow, but I can't place it," the detective said. "Try checking my criminal file."

After a hasty conference with his operative, Sam Radley, Mr Hardy added, "Son, the way things are popping there in Bayport, I think Sam had better fly back and help you boys with your investigation. I'll get hold of Jack Wayne. He should be able to land Sam there by midnight."

"Okay, Dad. We'll meet Sam at the airport."

After signing off, Frank and Joe hurried upstairs to their father's study. A thorough check of his file revealed no criminal listed under the name of Darrow.

"Dad must've been mistaken," Joe concluded.

Mrs Hardy and Aunt Gertrude were watching a film on television. The brothers joined them.

"I suppose you boys would like a snack," their aunt said after the programme ended.

"We wouldn't object," Frank replied with a grin.

As Miss Hardy went out to the kitchen, Joe suddenly remembered the coin he had picked up near the mansion window. As he examined it the young sleuth gave a cry of excitement.

"Frank! Take a look at this!"

The coin appeared to be a brass lucky piece. On both sides it bore the design of a dragon!

"Wow! The same design Chet saw on that tiled square!" Frank exclaimed.

The boys began to discuss their new clue excitedly. Mrs Hardy also looked at the lucky piece and pointed out the design of a violet above the dragon's head. Soon Aunt Gertrude returned to the living room, carrying a tray of sandwiches, biscuits and milk. She, too, became curious and asked to see the brass coin.

"Why, this belonged to old Jerome Perth!" she announced triumphantly.

"How do you know?" Joe asked.

"From the design—that's how," Aunt Gertrude retorted. "It was his personal trademark."

"Aunty, you're wonderful!" Frank exclaimed.

"That swindling old reprobate used to hand out these pieces right and left," she went on. "Especially when anyone asked him to contribute to charity! Used to say these would bring the holder luck, which was more important than money." Miss Hardy sniffed. "The dragon was appropriate!"

"Well, since this is the design Chet described—the one he saw on the tiled square—we know he didn't imagine it," Joe said to Frank.

"But we still don't know its purpose," Frank pointed out.

Mrs Hardy and Aunt Gertrude were keenly interested when they heard of Chet's experience. Mrs Hardy puckered her brow thoughtfully. "Gertrude, wasn't there once a summerhouse near the Perth mansion?" she asked.

"I believe there was, Laura. Seems to me it fell into neglect and was torn down. Why?"

"I was just wondering if that tiled surface might have been the floor of the summerhouse."

Joe snapped his fingers excitedly. "I'll bet you've hit it, Mother!" he exclaimed.

Frank nodded in agreement. "But in that case, why couldn't we find it this morning?" he mused.

Before anyone could answer, the TV late news came on. "A bulletin just handed to me," said the newscaster, "states that a daring jewel robbery was pulled in Chicago at ten o'clock tonight. More than one hundred thousand dollars' worth of uncut gems were stolen from the Spyker Jewellery Company. No further details as yet."

"Wow! That phone tip of Dad's *must* have been a fake one!" Joe exploded. "I'll bet Strang wanted to make sure Dad was safely sidetracked on Long Island before the gang pulled this new job!"

Frank sprang to his feet. "Come on, Joe! We can do some more detective work tonight!"

·7·

A Fast Fade-out

"WHAT do you have in mind, Frank?" Joe asked.

"You weren't sure Noel Strang was one of those men at the mansion tonight," Frank explained, "but we do know we saw him this morning."

"So?"

"If he was involved in this latest jewel robbery, he must have *flown* to Chicago. It's the only way he could have reached there in time. Maybe we can check that out at the airport."

"Smart idea!" Joe agreed. "Wait—I'll get the photo of Strang—we can use it if we need to ask the airlines' personnel whether or not they've seen him."

The Hardys reached the airport a few minutes before twelve. Joe said, "Let's start by checking the passenger lists for today's flights to Chicago."

"Strang wouldn't have used his own name if he were en route to commit a crime," Frank objected.

"Maybe not, but how about one of his aliases?" Joe pointed to a paper with typewritten data pasted on the reverse side of Strang's photo.

"Hey! That's a thought!"

At each of the airline desks, the boys asked to see passenger lists for all flights to Chicago since that morning. Neither Strang's name nor any of his known aliases was listed.

Joe showed one desk clerk the photo of Strang, but the man shook his head. "All the airline employees who are here now came on duty within the last hour." Then he pointed to a porter who was lounging near a flight gate. "You might ask that fellow over there. And try Benny at the newsstand."

"Thanks. We'll do that."

The boys showed their photograph to the porter and the newsstand operator. Neither recalled seeing such a man.

"How about charter flights?" Joe asked. "Let's check on that at the information desk."

The attendant on duty told the boys that they would have to inquire about this at the control tower. "That's where the flight plans are filed," he explained.

Before the Hardys could visit the tower, Joe spotted a plane coming in. "*Skyhappy Sal!*" he exclaimed.

This was a charter ship of the Ace Air Service, operated by Jack Wayne. Jack was a veteran pilot who often flew assignments for Fenton Hardy. The brothers were soon shaking hands with Jack and his passenger, Sam Radley.

"Good flight?" Joe asked the wiry investigator.

Sam nodded. "Fast and smooth. Your dad thought you boys might brief me right away so we can plan some action."

"We can start now," Frank told him, then gave an account of the events that had taken place in Bayport. He told of the jewel robbery in Chicago, and added, "Joe and I were about to ask the tower if Strang might have taken off for Chicago on a charter flight."

"I can do that," Jack offered. "I know the dispatcher."

"Good," said Frank. "Here's a photo of Strang—one of the men in the tower may recognize him, if he took a special flight out of here today. In the meantime, there's something the rest of us can be doing."

"What's that?" Radley asked.

"Check the airport parking place and see if Strang's foreign sports car is here."

"Good thinking, Frank," Radley said approvingly. "Your dad will tell you that a smart detective never takes anything for granted."

While Jack Wayne started off to the control tower, the Hardys and Sam Radley headed for the parking area. Although it was now past midnight, there were still several cars in the park.

As Sam and the boys began their inspection tour, a man stepped into view from between two rows of parked cars. Bull-necked and powerfully built, he had crew-cut hair and was wearing a loud sports jacket. At sight of the detectives, he hastily turned and retreated.

Sam Radley was startled. "That was Duke Makin!" he whispered.

"The racketeer and con man?" Joe asked, having heard his father mention the name.

"Yes," Sam replied. "I wonder what he's doing here." His sleuthing instincts aroused, the detective strode forward to investigate. Frank and Joe followed eagerly.

Suddenly an engine roared and a car came zooming out of the darkness. Sam and the Hardys had to leap out of the way as it screeched past!

"That's Strang's sports car!" Frank shouted.

Makin was hunched at the wheel. A figure appeared

to be huddled in the space behind the front seat, but the car whizzed by too quickly for a clear view. It swung out on to the road.

"Come on! Let's follow him!" Frank urged.

The Hardys and Radley ran to the boys' convertible, leaped in, and took off. But the chase seemed hopeless from the start. Makin, speeding recklessly, already was out of sight.

Frank flung the convertible along for a few miles, but after they had passed several crossroads and side roads, all three agreed to abandon the pursuit as hopeless. Glumly, Frank headed back to the airport.

"What do you suppose Makin was up to, Sam?" he queried. "Think he could be in with Strang on the jewel robberies?"

Radley frowned and shrugged. "Must be some kind of tie-up, if he's using Strang's car. Trouble is, we don't even know for sure that Strang's involved in the robberies."

"Looked to me as if someone was hiding in the car," Joe remarked. "Maybe that was Strang himself, trying not to be spotted."

"Could be," Radley agreed. "But if so, why was he hanging around the airport parking area at this time of night?"

When they arrived back at the airfield, Jack Wayne had important news. A charter plane—owned and piloted by a man named Al Hirff—had taken off at 9.37 P.M. The flight plan listed its destination as Chicago, and the aircraft was carrying a passenger named Norbert Smith.

"One of the tower operators was down on the field at the time," Jack went on, "and he saw the passenger getting aboard. He says the fellow looked just like this photograph of Strang!"

"Now we're getting somewhere!" Joe exclaimed. "For one thing, Strang wasn't the fellow hiding in his own car."

"Do you know this man Hirff?" Frank asked Jack.

"I've seen him," the pilot replied. "He rented hangar space here about a week before I flew Sam down to Florida."

"Jack," said Radley, "could you stick around here and let us know when the plane gets back?"

The pilot nodded. "Sure. I have a bunk in the office. Maybe I can get chummy with Hirff and pick up some information for you."

"Good idea," said Frank. "One thing more, Jack— keep an eye out for a black foreign sports car with a dented boot. It may come here to pick up Strang when he gets back."

"Wilco!" the pilot promised.

Radley was to sleep in the Hardys' guest room overnight. As they drove home, the boys discussed the situation with him.

"The plane took off at 9.37," Joe mused. "And the robbery took place at ten o'clock. It's a cinch Strang couldn't have made it to Chicago in time to pull the job!"

"Maybe he planned it that way," Frank reasoned, "so he'd have a clear alibi in case his movements were checked. He could have had confederates steal the jewels. Then Strang showed up in Chicago immediately afterwards to take charge of the loot and give the robbers a fast lift out of town."

"You may have the answer," Radley agreed.

When they arrived home, Mrs Hardy greeted them with the news that her husband had radioed again. "He heard about the Chicago jewel robbery just after you left Long Island, Sam. He wants you to contact him at once."

Radley and the boys hurried downstairs and warmed up the transmitter. Soon Fenton Hardy's voice came over the speaker. Frank and Joe quickly reported the latest developments.

"Great work, sons!" the detective congratulated them. "This is the first solid clue we've had that may link Strang with the jewel thefts."

"Want us to have him picked up for questioning if he comes back to Bayport?" Frank asked, taking the microphone from Joe.

"No, the local police would have no jurisdiction. Anyway, they'd need a warrant from Chicago," Mr Hardy replied. "Besides, unless Strang were foolish enough to be carrying the loot with him—which I'm sure he isn't—we still have no real evidence against him. Until we do, there's no sense in showing our hand."

"How about me, Fenton?" Sam Radley put in.

"I'll probably need your help to cover all the angles in Chicago. Tell you what, Sam. If Strang is back in Bayport by eight tomorrow morning, stay there and work with the boys. Otherwise, hop on the eight-thirty commercial flight to Chicago and I'll meet you at O'Hare Airport. Tell Jack to stick around and give the boys a hand."

Radley breakfasted early with the Hardys next morning, then the brothers took him to the airport. Hirff's plane still had not returned, so Radley boarded the eight-thirty flight to Chicago.

Frank and Joe drove home and looked up Duke
Makin in their father's crime file. They learned that
Makin had served time on three different convictions,
and recently had been released from Sing Sing. Since
then, so far as the dossier showed, no charge was
pending against him.

Next, Frank called an estate agent who was a friend
of Mr Hardy's and learned that the Perth estate had
been handled by a solicitor named Cyrus Lamkin. The
boys drove to his office.

Lamkin sat at an old-fashioned roll-top desk. He was
a podgy white-haired man, whose waistcoat was littered
with cigar ash. "You're the Hardy boys, eh?" he said,
rising to shake hands. "Fine man, your father! What
can I do for you?"

Frank asked guardedly if he could tell them the
present status of the Perth mansion.

"Why, I sold that just a few months ago," Lamkin
replied. "Good price, too. I imagine the owners were
glad to get that white elephant off their hands! They're
distant relatives of the original owner. Live out in
Ohio."

"Who bought it?" Joe asked.

"Man named Aden Darrow." Frank and Joe gave a
start of surprise as Lamkin went on, "He's rather
quick-tempered, but a very brilliant man apparently.
Used to be a professor at Western State University."

The Hardys looked at each other in amazement. Why
would a college professor associate with a known crook
like Strang?

Lamkin went on, "Funny how a piece of property
can suddenly arouse interest in the market," he mused
conversationally. "Take that Perth place. Vacant for

years. Then Darrow comes along and buys it. And now you lads are asking about the place. Second inquiry I've had in just a few days."

"You mean someone else besides us has been asking about it?" Frank inquired.

"Yes, a prospective tenant came in the other day. He wanted to rent it."

"Someone local?" Joe asked.

"No, from New York," Lamkin paused to consult his calendar pad. "A Mr Delius Martin."

Again Frank and Joe were startled. The name was one of Duke Makin's aliases!

After a short further conversation with Mr Lamkin, the boys thanked the solicitor and went out to their convertible.

"What do you make of it, Frank?" Joe said.

"Nothing—the puzzle's getting more complicated all the time. A college prof rents the place, a notorious jewel thief moves in with him, and now we have to fit Makin in somewhere!"

The boys decided to check on Darrow's background. But first they drove to the repair dock to see how work was progressing on the *Sleuth*. The manager promised to have the boat ready in three days.

Frank and Joe spotted the *Napoli* moored nearby. They were hailed by Tony Prito, who suggested they all go for a brief swim.

"How about it?" Joe said, turning to his brother. "Our trunks are in the car."

"Okay with me!"

Tony took the *Napoli* down the bay a short distance and they anchored at a pleasant spot in a sheltered cove. A cabin cruiser lay at anchor not far away. Frank and Tony took a quick plunge, then climbed back aboard to sunbathe. Joe continued swimming by himself.

Like a seal, Joe cut his way down through the cool, refreshing water. Then he swirled back towards the surface.

Suddenly he felt himself siezed from underneath. A brawny arm clamped itself around his neck in a choking grip and pulled him down!

·8·

Rock Hounds' Shadow

JOE struggled desperately. He had already used up most of the air in his lungs even before he was attacked. Now he was being gripped beneath the surface, unable to call or signal for help!

Joe kicked and threshed, but he could not free himself from his attacker's iron grip. The only result was a tightening of pressure against his Adam's apple and a vicious jab in the ribs. When Joe tried to squirm round to face his assailant, the man rolled with him.

Joe's lungs were soon near the bursting point. If only he could reach the surface!

Aboard the *Napoli*, Frank began to worry. "What's Joe doing down there?" he muttered.

"Maybe he met a mermaid," Tony quipped lazily.

As Frank scanned the waters, he noticed an uprush of air bubbles about a hundred yards away. Wordlessly, he plunged over the side.

Cutting his way downward, Frank peered intently through the wavering transparent greenness. His heart pounded at what he saw. Joe was helpless in the grip of a goggled frogman!

As Frank stroked swiftly towards them, the frogman released his victim and swam off.

"Good grief! I hope I'm not too late!" Frank thought frantically.

64

Joe was limp, his head sagging as he slowly floated upwards. Frank grabbed him under the arms and hauled him upwards.

"Tony! Give us a hand!" Frank shouted as he broke the surface.

Tony had been watching anxiously for a sight of the Hardy boys. At Frank's call, he sent the *Napoli* gliding towards them. In a few moments they had Joe safely aboard.

"Get back to the dock! Fast!" Frank exclaimed. He positioned Joe as best he could in the bottom of the boat and quickly began applying mouth-to-mouth resuscitation.

The *Napoli* went planing over the water towards shore. The bouncing made Frank's efforts doubly difficult, but by bracing himself against the side he managed to hold Joe fairly steady.

Tony cut the engine and yelled for help as he brought the boat alongside the dock. Four men assisted the boys in lifting Joe out of the *Napoli*, then laid him full length on the dock. Frank quickly resumed mouth-to-mouth resuscitation.

"I've called an ambulance!" someone shouted.

But Joe was already reviving. Frank breathed a silent prayer of thanks.

"Boy! You sure had a close call!" Tony said, squatting down beside Joe.

"You're telling me." Joe grinned weakly. "I must've swallowed half of Barmet Bay!"

By the time the ambulance arrived, Joe was on his feet. He allowed the doctor to examine him but refused to be taken to the hospital.

"Nothing doing. I'm okay," he insisted.

"Well, I can't force you." The doctor grinned and turned to Frank. "At least take him home and put him to bed for a while."

Once they were seated in the convertible and the ambulance had departed, Joe protested, "Listen, I'm not sleepy! Why should I go to bed?" he argued. "Then we'd have to tell Mom what happened. And think of the fuss Aunt Gertrude would make!"

"Okay, if you're sure you feel all right."

As the boys walked back to the dock, Joe said, "The frogman who attacked me must have come from that cabin cruiser in the cove."

"I think that cruiser pulled out before Frank and I started sunbathing," Tony objected.

"Joe could still be right. The cruiser could have left and arranged to pick up the frogman somewhere else," Frank pointed out. "It's a cinch he couldn't have been lurking on shore, just waiting for us to show up. We didn't even know, ourselves, that we'd be going to that particular spot to swim."

"I suppose you're right," Tony agreed, frowning thoughtfully. "Must've been just bad luck. The cruiser spotted us, and whoever was aboard decided this was a perfect chance to nail at least one of the Hardys."

The boys boarded the *Napoli* and made a quick scouting trip back to the cove. The cruiser was nowhere in sight. Neither Tony nor the Hardys had paid enough attention to the craft to be able to identify it. Nor had Frank seen the frogman clearly enough to provide the police with a useful description.

The boys dressed aboard the *Napoli* and headed back to the dock. Frank and Joe then said goodbye to Tony and drove home. Chet Morton's tomato-red jalopy was parked in front of the house. A girl was seated in one of the porch rocking-chairs.

"That's Iola!" Joe exclaimed as they drove up.

She came running to meet them as they got out of the car. "Oh, thank goodness!" Iola said excitedly. "I was afraid you might not get back in time!"

"Something wrong?" Frank asked.

"I think we've found the man who stole our amethyst —at least we think we know where he is!"

"Where?" Joe exclaimed.

Iola explained that she, Callie, and Chet had gone rock hunting again that morning in the hills outside Bayport. While they were trying to locate the spot where the girls had picked up the amethyst, they had glimpsed a man trailing them at a distance.

"Did he look like the fellow who questioned you at the gem shop?" Frank put in.

"He was skulking too far behind—and ducking out of sight whenever we looked back," Iola said, "so we couldn't be sure."

"Where are Chet and Callie?" Joe asked.

"They stayed behind. We made a fire and now they're having lunch—acting as if nothing's wrong. But Chet told me to sneak back to the car and get you two."

"Okay. Hop in your jalopy and lead the way," Frank said. "We'll follow you."

Iola drove into the hills west of Bayport. Frank and Joe stayed close behind in their convertible. Finally the jalopy pulled off the road. The Hardys parked nearby.

"We'll have to do some walking," Iola said.

A five-minute hike brought them to a hill over-looking a narrow ravine. Iola explained that Chet and Callie were waiting just beyond. "And the man who's been shadowing us is down there somewhere among all those rocks and shrubs—at least, he was when I left to get you."

"A perfect set-up," Joe gloated. "Frank, suppose you and I go into the ravine at this end and flush him out? Then he'll either have to break for high ground or go right out past Chet."

Frank agreed to the plan, and the boys wound their way down the hillside and up the floor of the ravine. Iola headed along the brow of the hill to rejoin Chet and Callie.

The Hardys spread out, searching among the brush and boulders. Twenty minutes later they emerged at the opposite end of the small canyon, their faces registering disappointment. Chet and the girls ran to meet them.

"Did you find him?" Chet asked.

Frank shook his head. "No, but there are signs he was there."

"We spotted a trail of broken brush where someone climbed out of the ravine," Joe added.

Chet's moonface sagged. "Rats! I thought sure we could nab him!"

"I'll bet he guessed that Iola went for help," Callie put in, "so he decided he'd better not stay around."

The Hardys drove home, eager to tackle their investigation of Aden Darrow. Mrs Hardy informed them that Jack Wayne had telephoned from the airport. Frank called him back.

"Strang landed about an hour ago," Jack reported. "I tried to reach you, but couldn't."

"Anyone with him?" Frank inquired eagerly.

"Just the pilot, Al Hirff. That black sports car didn't show up, but another car did. A tough-looking guy met them and drove off with Strang."

"What about Hirff?"

"Still here at the airport. I tried to strike up a conversation with him, but no luck."

"Good work, Jack," Frank said. "Keep trying."

Frank passed the news to Joe. The boys ate a quick lunch of sandwiches and lemon pie, and then prepared to book a long-distance call to Western State University. Before they could do so, the telephone rang. Joe answered.

"This is Mr Filmer at the gem shop," said the voice at the other end.

"Oh, yes, Mr Filmer. Is anything wrong?"

"Well, a man came into my shop a while ago with three stones that he wanted me to appraise. I don't know what sort of mystery you boys are working on, but I thought you might want to know—the stones were amethysts!"

·9·

Secret Cruiser

JOE's pulse quickened when he heard of this promising new lead. "We'll be right over to talk to you, Mr Filmer!" he exclaimed.

Hanging up, he told Frank what the gem shop proprietor had said.

"Maybe we're on to something," Frank agreed.

Aunt Gertrude paused in the midst of trimming a pie crust as they rushed out through the kitchen door. "Good gracious! Where are you boys off to now?" she scolded. "Don't you realize you'll ruin your digestions?"

"On your cooking? Why, Aunty!" Joe grinned and ducked out before she could retort.

The boys hopped into their convertible and drove to the shop on Bay Street. Although Mr Filmer again looked somewhat nervous, and obviously had no desire to become involved in a criminal case, he seemed eager to be helpful.

"This man who brought the stones—had you ever seen him before?" Frank inquired.

"No, and he gave no name," Mr Filmer replied. "The amethysts were uncut stones—quite large."

"Genuine?"

"Oh, yes, indeed."

"Did you ask where he got them?" Joe put in.

"Well, I tried to find out where they came from, but he was very evasive. And he wouldn't leave the stones for cutting and polishing, although I offered to do it very reasonably."

"What did this fellow look like?" Frank asked.

"Oh, he was big and husky." The proprietor's Adam's apple bobbed as if the thought made him uneasy. "And he was dressed rather sportily. His hair was bushy and he had on a checked sports jacket."

Frank darted a surprised glance at Joe. The description matched!

"Sounds like Duke Makin," Joe muttered. Hoping for a further lead, he asked Mr Filmer, "Did you see what kind of car he was driving?"

"I don't think he came in a car," the proprietor replied, "although someone may have dropped him off, I suppose. But I watched when he left and I saw him get into a taxi at that stand across the street."

"How long ago was that?" Frank asked.

"*Mmm*, say half an hour."

"Thanks, Mr Filmer! You've been a big help!"

"Don't mention it, boys."

Frank and Joe hurried across the street. A taxi driver was slouched in his cab, reading a newspaper. The boys described Makin to him and asked the man if he had seen which driver had taken him away.

"That was Mike, I think. Should be back here soon, unless he picked up another fare."

The Hardys returned to their convertible to wait. They fidgeted impatiently as twenty minutes went by. At last another taxi pulled into the stance. The first driver looked up from his paper, gave the boys a two-fingered whistle, and jerked his thumb towards the other taxi. Frank and Joe strode across the street and questioned the man who had just arrived.

"Sure, I know the guy you mean," he told them. "I took him out to some little picnic ground in Shore Road."

"*Picnic* ground?" Joe echoed in surprise.

"Yeah, it did seem like a funny place for him to get out," the driver said. "I thought he probably planned to meet someone there."

At Frank's request, the driver described the spot and sketched a map. Frank tipped him, and the boys hurried back to their own car.

"Let's take a look at the place right now," Joe proposed. "We might pick up a clue."

"Right!" Frank took the wheel and soon their convertible was rolling along Shore Road.

In a few minutes they came to the spot the driver had described, a small clearing laid out for picnickers. A family was eating at one of the tables. Otherwise, the site was deserted.

The Hardys got out to look around. Beyond the clearing, the ground was wooded and sloped steeply down to the shore of Barmet Bay.

"I wonder what Makin was doing around here," Joe said.

"He must have had *some* reason," Frank said. "Maybe we can find it."

The two boys wandered around the fringes of the picnic area, peering among the trees and shrubbery. Suddenly Joe gasped and pointed towards the water.

"Look, Frank!"

Far below, and about a hundred yards to seaward

from the point of the bay at which they were standing, the shore was indented by a reedy inlet. A cabin cruiser lay anchored close to shore.

"Oh—oh! I'll bet that's the answer, all right," Frank agreed. "Maybe it's the same cruiser the frogman came from!"

The Hardys scrambled along the brow of the slope until they were overlooking the inlet. Even here the cruiser was not completely visible. Its hull was screened by heavy clumps of reed and rushes, and the boys' view was further blocked by the thick growth cresting the slope.

"Certainly picked a good place to hide," Joe muttered. "Let's go down closer."

The Hardys began picking their way cautiously down the steep hillside. But as the trees and brush thinned out, they themselves were exposed to view as they moved close to the cruiser. Suddenly they saw a man emerge from the cabin and throw back one arm.

"Look out!" Frank cried out. "That may be a bomb he's throwing!"

The boys flattened themselves in the underbrush as an object spun through the air. . . . *Whoosh!*

"A gas grenade!" Joe yelled to his brother. The boys sprang to their feet and hurried back up the slope as the throb of a boat engine reached their ears. In seconds the hillside was filled with billowing purple smoke!

Gasping, choking, and with tears streaming from their eyes, Frank and Joe finally reached the top of the hill and ran towards the picnic ground. The family at the table stared at them in wide-eyed excitement.

"What's happening?" the man shouted.

"Some prankster in a boat down there threw a tear-gas grenade," Frank said, so as not to alarm the group.

"Why, that's terrible! Someone should call the police!" the man's wife said.

"We'll report it," Frank promised.

Fortunately, an off shore breeze was blowing the smoke away from the picnic ground and out on to the bay. But the smoke screen hid the cruiser completely from view.

The Hardys hurried to their car and warmed up the short-wave set. Frank contacted the Coast Guard station and the radio operator on duty promised that an effort would be made to spot the cabin cruiser. There seemed little hope of identifying it, however, among all the other craft on the bay, especially since the boys had noticed no special features, not even the cruiser's name.

Frank and Joe were glum as they drove home. "Do you suppose Makin was aboard?" Joe asked.

Frank shrugged and frowned uncertainly. "I don't know. That inlet was practically a swamp—it certainly didn't look like an easy place to get on or off the cruiser. But the purple smoke was the same kind we ran into the other night. That would seem to link the cruiser itself to Strang."

Joe glanced at his brother. "Incidentally, why did you ask Mr Filmer if those amethysts were genuine?"

"Makin's a confidence man plus his other rackets—remember? I thought he might be planning to use the stones for some con game."

As soon as the brothers arrived home, Frank booked a call to Western State University. He explained that he wanted information about a former professor named Aden Darrow.

"I'll connect you with Dean Gibbs," the switchboard operator replied.

Frank identified himself to the dean.

"Oh, yes. I've often heard of your father," Gibbs said. "What can I do for you?"

Frank explained that Darrow's name had come up in connection with a case the Hardys were investigating. He asked if the dean could tell him anything about Darrow's background.

"Up until last term, Professor Darrow taught a special course in crime-detection methods here," Dean Gibbs replied. "He has a background in both physical and organic chemistry. Before he joined our faculty, he worked in police crime labs in several western cities."

"Why did he leave the university?"

"Well, that was rather unfortunate," Gibbs said. "You see, he had been trying to raise funds for research on a project which he claimed would be of great value to the police."

"What sort of project?" Frank inquired.

"To be honest, we know very little about it. Professor Darrow had become secretive and suspicious. In fact, we felt he was on the verge of a nervous breakdown. After the school refused to allot any money for his project, Darrow became extremely upset and resigned."

"I see." Frank was thoughtful for a moment, then said, "We were told he recently bought a house here in Bayport. Did he say what his plans were when he left the university?"

"No, not a word. In fact, we had no idea of his present whereabouts before you called."

Frank was just hanging up when a plane roared low over the house. The boys could hear it turn and zoom back as if it were buzzing the Hardy residence.

"That may be Jack Wayne!" Joe exclaimed. He rushed to look out of the window. "It's *Skyhappy Sal*, all right. Maybe Jack wants to talk to us!"

The boys dashed downstairs and switched on their two-way radio. Joe took the microphone.

"Hardys to *Sal*. . . . Can you read us?"

The pilot's voice crackled over the speaker, "Loud and clear, Joe! Listen, I think I've picked up a hot lead from Hirff. It may tie in with those jewel robberies your dad is—"

Jack's voice was drowned by a sudden burst of static. When it came through again, it was so faint the Hardys could catch only a few words:

"If the tigers bite . . . amethyst . . ."

There was another burst of static. The radio message died out completely!

· 10 ·

The Ghostly Figure

JOE tuned the receiver anxiously, trying to restore a clear signal.

"Hardys to *Sal*! Come in, please! . . . Hardys calling *Sal*!"

There was no response. The two boys looked at each other, worried and mystified.

"What do you suppose went wrong with the transmission, Joe?" his brother muttered.

"Search me. What I'm wondering is whether Jack's okay!"

The brothers ran up the basement stairs and dashed outdoors. Shading their eyes, they scanned the sky. Jack's plane was now a mere speck in the blue, rapidly dwindling from sight. It was heading on a southerly course.

"At least he's still up there!" Frank said, half under his breath.

Joe added. "Let's hope he makes it all the way—wherever it is he's going!"

The boys went indoors and tried for a while longer to re-establish radio contact with *Skyhappy Sal*, but their efforts were unsuccessful. They returned to the living room and slumped into comfortable chairs.

"I'd sure like to know what Jack was trying to tell us," Frank brooded.

"So would I. That message was weird!" Joe furrowed

his brow, trying to make sense out of the few words that had filtered through. "*If the tigers bite . . .* What could he possibly have been referring to, Frank?"

"Don't ask me. It's strictly Greek as far as I'm concerned." Frank scowled in deep thought. " 'Tigers' might refer to animals in some zoo, I suppose. Or maybe to tigers being brought into the country by some animal importer."

Joe shook his head. "Sounds pretty far-fetched. Jack was flying south. That *might* mean he was heading for the Caribbean area."

"Maybe. So what?"

"Well, they have jaguars down in Central America. And, in Spanish, the jaguar is called *tigre.*"

"For that matter, what about tiger sharks?" Frank broke off abruptly and sprang up from his chair. "Wait a minute! We must be getting balmy with the heat. We can find out where Jack's going just by checking with the airport tower!"

Frank strode to the telephone in the front hall and dialled. He talked for a few moments, then hung up and returned to the living room, wearing a frustrated expression.

"The tower operator says Jack didn't file a flight plan—which probably means he's just making a brief local flight."

"Then we should be hearing from him soon," Joe suggested.

"We hope!" Frank added, crossing his fingers.

Just then a car pulled up in front of the house with a squeal of tyres and a series of loud backfires.

"Don't tell me—let me guess. It's Chet Morton," said Frank.

Joe grinned and glanced out of the window at Chet's red jalopy. "Who else?" He went to open the front door as their chunky friend came bounding up the path. "Hi, Hercules! How'd you make out on the amethyst trail?" Joe asked.

"We didn't." Chet went on into the living room and flopped on to the settee. "Those girls still can't remember where they picked up the stone—and we didn't find any new ones, either."

"Tough luck," Frank sympathized.

The Hardys gave Chet news of the latest developments, including Jack Wayne's radio message.

"Tigers?" Chet's eyes bulged. "I hope you're not going to be bumping into any of *those* on this case!" He paused to sniff the aroma wafting from the kitchen. "*Mmm!* Do I smell chicken?"

"Fried chicken." Mrs Hardy had paused at the door and smiled as she glanced in. "And there'll be honey to go with Aunt Gertrude's hot biscuits. Would you like to have dinner with us, Chet?"

"*Would* I? Boy, but yes! But I'd better call Mom and let her know."

An hour later, the meal just over, the doorbell rang. Frank went to answer it.

"Telegram for Frank and Joe Hardy," said a messenger.

Frank signed for it and ripped open the yellow envelope as he brought it into the living room.

"Hey! It's from Dean Gibbs at Western State University!" He read the telegram aloud:

PROFESSOR DARROW'S SISTER EAGER TO FIND
HIM. IF POSSIBLE PLEASE CONTACT PROFESSOR.
ASK HIM TO CALL HER.

"Wow! What a break!" Joe exploded.

Chet looked puzzled. "How do you make that out?"

"This gives us a perfect excuse to go right up to the Perth mansion and find out what's going on!" Frank explained. "Want to come along?"

"Well, I dunno." Chet squirmed uncomfortably. "Maybe you'd better count me out."

"Don't be chicken. You're coming with us!" Joe said, slapping the plump youth on the back.

Frank said, "I've just thought of something. If Professor Darrow taught crime-detection methods, maybe we can find some articles by him in Dad's journals. That'll give us material to work up a conversation with him. It might even furnish us with a clue to his research project!"

"Good idea!" Joe agreed enthusiastically.

In their father's study the Hardys checked the annual index of each of the three criminology journals to which their father subscribed. They could find only one article written by Aden Darrow. It dealt with new data on the power of light beams.

Although the article gave no hint of Darrow's present field of research, it did include a photograph of the professor demonstrating some ultra-violet equipment. He wore spectacles and was bald, with a rumpled fringe of grey hair.

"Well, at least we know what he looks like," Joe remarked.

The boys hurried to the Hardys' convertible. A red glow of sunset suffused the western sky as they drove out of Bayport's residential district and into the wooded outskirts of town. Soon they pulled up on the lane directly in front of the Perth mansion.

"You fellows handle it," Chet said. "I'll stay in the car."

Grinning, Frank and Joe walked up the tree-covered slope to the house. Joe pressed the doorbell. Moments passed. He was about to ring again when the door suddenly opened. A tall, dark-haired, hatchet-faced man confronted them.

Noel Strang!

"Well, what do you want?" he demanded, giving the boys a hard stare.

"We have a message for the man who lives here," Frank said boldly.

"*I* live here," Strang retorted. "What is it?"

"We mean Professor Aden Darrow," Frank said, displaying the telegram.

Strang reached out to take it, but Frank made no effort to give him the paper. "Sorry, but the message is personal. It's from his sister."

"Too bad!" Strang snapped. "Professor Darrow suffered a breakdown from overwork and had to leave on a long vacation. I have no idea how to reach him."

"Did he go out of the country?" Joe spoke up. "If so, maybe we could—"

The door slammed in the boys' faces!

Frank and Joe looked at each other uncertainly, then turned and started down the veranda steps. In the gathering dust a light suddenly blazed on in an upstairs window. Joe glanced up over his shoulder, then clutched Frank's arm.

"Look!" he exclaimed.

Through the window curtain, they glimpsed a man who seemed to resemble Professor Darrow! An instant later he moved out of sight.

"Strang's probably watching us," Frank muttered. "Let's go!"

At the car they discussed their next move.

"Let's drive around till it gets dark, and then come back and keep watch on that window," Joe suggested.

"Okay," Frank agreed.

Leaving the lane, the boys cruised back and forth along the main road until darkness had closed in. Then they returned and parked their convertible well out of sight of the house. Taking torches, the boys started up the slope. Chet was not enthusiastic but agreed to accompany them.

Suddenly Frank paused as moonlight glinted off something on the ground. He switched on his torch cautiously, covering the lens with his fingers to shade the glow.

There lay the square tiled surface Chet had described to them! The dragon design was formed in coloured mosaic.

"That's it!" Chet whispered excitedly.

"How is it we couldn't find it before?" Joe said.

"Maybe sometimes it's covered over with brush and loose shrubbery—on purpose," Frank reasoned.

Before they could examine the spot more closely, Chet gasped and pointed off to the left. A white figure was moving slowly among the trees!

"It's that spook again!" Joe exclaimed. "This time, let's nail him!"

Chet moved his lips in speechless terror, but rather than be left behind, he went lumbering off after the two Hardys.

Frank and Joe sprinted straight towards the ghostly figure, determined not to let it elude them a second time. But the phantom had already seen them and went darting off like a vanishing wisp of mist.

The pursuit circled and zigzagged about the mansion grounds. Chet soon lost all fear as he became convinced that the fleeing spectre was only flesh and blood. He joined in the chase with zest, his sturdy legs pumping as if he were pursuing a rival team's player on the Bayport High football field.

Frank was in the lead, with the other two boys on either side searching swiftly among the trees.

"Joe! Can you see him?" Frank called back. "I think he went that way!"

There was no answer. Frank glanced over his shoulder, then gasped.

Joe had disappeared!

A Parcel of Gems

FRANK skidded to a halt and peered intently through the darkness. "Joe!" he called in almost a whisper. "Joe! Where are you?"

Chet hurried to Frank's side. "What's wrong?" he asked anxiously.

"I don't know. Joe was only a few yards from me just a minute ago. Now I can't see him."

Chet glanced around. The white phantom had also disappeared—swallowed up in the gloom.

Suddenly Joe's muffled voice reached their ears. "This way, you guys! But watch your step! I fell down a hole!"

Frank and Chet hurried towards the sound, with Frank beaming his torch over the ground in front of them. Both boys stopped as the yellow glow revealed a large, square hole.

"Hey! There's that tiled thing!" Chet exclaimed. "But it's open!"

Frank saw that the whole tiled surface had flapped downwards. It was now hanging flush against one side of the hole, its coloured mosaic glistening in the light.

"I'm down here," called Joe. "That tiled square must be hinged like a trap door. Either its supports gave way, or someone must've opened it by remote control. And that's not all—there's a tunnel down here!"

Frank shone his torch down the hole. It was brick-walled and about twelve feet deep. In the side opposite the flap-down tiled surface was an opening just large enough for Joe to enter without stooping. Alongside this opening, a metal ladder was attached to the wall, for climbing in or out of the hole.

"Wow!" Chet dropped to his knees and peered below. "Where do you suppose that opening leads?"

"I'll bet there's a tunnel going all the way to the house," Joe answered, shining his own beam through the opening.

Frank told Chet of Mrs Hardy's theory that the tiled surface had been the floor of an old summerhouse. He added, "The summerhouse was probably built on purpose to hide this end of the tunnel.

"That's quite a drop," Frank continued anxiously. "Are you hurt, Joe?"

"No! I managed to break the fall. It was easy after some of those judo slams we've taken! Besides, this floor feels spongy. It must have been padded in case of an accident."

Frank peered in all directions. "Looks as though we've lost our spook for good."

"Then let's search this tunnel," Joe proposed.

Chet gulped uneasily. "How do you know what we'll find at the other end?"

"We don't. That's why we want to find out."

"B-b-but you said yourself that someone may have opened this by remote control," Chet said shakily. "How do we know the crooks aren't using the tunnel right now? And—and they may even be trying to lure us into a trap!"

Joe chuckled and aimed his torch into the tunnel

entrance. "There's some kind of phone in there, hanging on a hook—probably an intercom to the house. Want me to call and ask?"

Frank looked serious. "I think Chet has a point, Joe. Maybe one of us should stay here—*outside* the tunnel—in case of emergency."

"Okay, you two flip a coin. Me for the tunnel!"

Frank spun a coin, caught it, and slapped the coin on the back of his other hand. "Winner goes with Joe. You name it, Chet."

"Uh—well—heads."

Frank shone his beam on the coin. "Heads. Guess you're elected, Chet. But loo —you don't *have* to go! Why don't you stay here and I'll—"

"Nothing doing," Chet protested bravely. "I won the toss, so I'll go." With the look of a condemned man the podgy youth climbed down the metal ladder. He could smell the dank, musty passageway.

Joe was already inside the tunnel entrance. "Come on!" he called back over his shoulder.

As Chet followed Joe into the tunnel, his bulky form brushed the intercom phone off its hook. Instantly a red light flashed on, evidently a signal to indicate that the circuit was now "live"—no doubt a buzzer was ringing at the other end of the line!

Chet clutched Joe. They stared at the unit as if it were a rattlesnake about to strike.

Suddenly a voice crackled from the phone. "Hello. . . . *hello!*" Joe snatched up the instrument as the voice went on, "Is that you, Waxie?"

Joe responded in a curt, flat tone, "Yeah?"

"Well, what do you want now?" the voice inquired irritably. "What did you come back for?"

Joe glanced helplessly at Chet; then, snatching at the first inspiration that came into his head, he replied nasally, "Orders."

"Orders? What's the matter with you, Waxie? You gettin' absent-minded? The boss gave you all the dope —about the disappearing floor—" The voice broke off as if the speaker had suddenly become suspicious. "Wait a minute! What's going on out there? Who is this?"

Joe dropped the phone and gave Chet a shove. "Come on! Let's go!" he muttered urgently. "Now we've *really* stirred up a hornet's nest!"

The boys scrambled up the ladder and told Frank what had happened. All three ran for the car. In moments Frank was revving the engine and the convertible was roaring off down the lane.

"What a bad break!" Joe grumbled as they turned on to the main road.

"It was my fault," Chet admitted, "and I'm sorry. But I certainly learned something—namely, not to get mixed up in any more of your nutty cases! So next time count me out!"

The Hardys chuckled and Joe apologized for his remark. Between them, the two young sleuths managed to make Chet change his mind by telling him they could not get along without him.

The clock in the living room was just striking nine when Frank and Joe arrived home. A note propped on the dining room table explained that their mother and Aunt Gertrude had gone to visit a neighbour down the street.

The boys got apples and milk from the refrigerator. Frank poured two glasses and they sat down in the kitchen to discuss their case.

"Think we should notify the police?" Joe said.

"About Darrow?" Frank shrugged uneasily. "I don't know. We're not sure it was him that we saw. For all we know, he may have told Strang not to admit any visitors. Remember, Dean Gibbs said he had become very huffy."

Joe nodded. "I sure wish Dad or Sam Radley were here to advise us."

A moment later the radio signal buzzer sounded from the basement. "Maybe that's Dad now!" Joe exclaimed, setting down his glass and tossing his apple core into the rubbish bin.

The boys rushed downstairs and soon established radio contact with their father, who was calling from Chicago.

"Sam and I are still sifting leads here," Fenton Hardy reported. "The thieves seem to have covered their tracks pretty well. Incidentally, the same method was used as on all the other jobs. The private patrolman guarding the place blacked out and has no recollection of what happened."

The detective listened as Frank and Joe brought him up to date on events in Bayport. He, too, was baffled by Jack Wayne's interrupted radio message. When the boys asked what to do about the situation at the Perth mansion, he was silent for a moment, then said:

"That window at which you think you saw Darrow— was it barred or heavily screened in any way?"

"No, it was partly open," Joe replied.

"Then if the man was Darrow, it hardly sounds as if he's being held against his will. Strang undoubtedly has some kind of undercover set-up there at the mansion. Darrow may not be aware of it. And we still have no proof Strang's involved in these jewel thefts. Proof is what we need before we move in on him. Meantime, I have another job for you boys."

Mr Hardy explained that he had just received another anonymous phone tip. "The caller simply said 'Go to Haley Building—Bayport' and then hung up. Sounds to me like another fake lead, but I wish you boys would check it."

"We'll do it right away, Dad," Frank promised.

Two minutes later the brothers' convertible was speeding into the town. It pulled up in front of a new office building on Main Street.

An elderly night watchman was seated at a desk in the entrance hall. As Frank and Joe entered, he glanced up at the wall clock, which read 9.41.

"Kind o' late, you fellows. This place'll be closin' up in about twenty minutes—in fact, the building's practically empty now. Someone you wanted to see?"

When Frank showed his identification, the watchman's face brightened. "Oh, Fenton Hardy's boys, eh? Well, I'm pleased to meet you!"

Frank told why they had come and asked if anything unusual or suspicious had happened that evening. The watchman shook his head.

"No. Except a parcel o' gems was delivered to Paul Tiffman up on the fifth floor 'round eight-thirty. But I knew beforehand that was comin'. Tiffman's a diamond merchant, y'see. When he stays late like tonight to receive a delivery, he always tells me. Most nights, everyone's gone by six."

Both Frank and Joe had stiffened at the mention of gems. Before they could comment, the lift signal rang. The watchman rose.

" 'Scuse me, boys. I have to double as lift operator after six o'clock. That must be Tiffman now, wantin' to go home."

The Hardys asked to ride up. When the watchman opened the lift door on the fifth floor, they saw a worried-looking man, plump and dark-moustached. "Hasn't that messenger arrived yet?" he asked.

The watchman looked surprised. "Why sure, Mr Tiffman. He was here at eight-thirty. I took him up, and then brought him down again later after he delivered those gems to you."

Tiffman's jaw dropped open. "Are you crazy?" he spluttered. "I haven't received any gems. No one has come to my office this evening!"

·12·

The "Seacat" Clue

THE watchman stared at the diamond merchant. Both their faces were turning an angry crimson.

"Mr Tiffman, I don't know what kind of a joke you're playin'," the watchman said, "but I saw that messenger with my own eyes!"

"And I don't know, Mike, what kind of a joke *you're* playing!" Tiffman roared back. "I tell you no messenger came to my office!"

"Can't help that! He came here and left!"

"I think you'd better call the police at once," Frank put in quietly.

"Who are you?" Tiffman snapped.

"We're sons of Fenton Hardy, the private detective." Frank explained about the anonymous phone tip. Tiffman's attitude promptly changed.

The watchman called the police. A patrol car was at the building within moments, and Chief Collig arrived a few minutes later, accompanied by a plain-clothes detective.

"You boys watch the door," Collig told the two patrol car officers. "The rest of you come upstairs to Mr Tiffman's office."

The five crowded into the lift and went up. Tiffman's office door was flush-panelled with a pane

91

in one corner. It was marked "507" in modernistic metal numbers, and the name plate below said: PAUL TIFFMAN, *Gemologist*.

After the Hardys had told Collig about the anonymous tip-off and the two men had told their stories, the police chief commented, "Sounds to me as if that messenger pulled a fast one."

"You mean he simply walked off without delivering the gems?" When Collig nodded, Tiffman frowned and shook his head. "That doesn't make sense. If he were planning to flee with the diamonds, why bother coming to Bayport at all?"

"Is there any chance he could have been waylaid between the lift and this office?" Joe put in. "If so, the thug might have dragged his body somewhere out of sight, and then gone down in the lift posing as the messenger."

Collig turned to Mike. "How about it? You sure the man you took down was the same man you brought up here?"

"Sure was," the watchman said tartly, "unless he was awful good at disguises. That messenger had red hair, freckles, and a wart on his cheek. So did the man who rode down."

"Have you ever seen this messenger?" Collig asked Tiffman.

"Wouldn't know him from Adam."

"Who sent him?"

Tiffman named a firm of diamond importers in New York City.

"Ever had deliveries from them before?"

Once again Tiffman shook his head. "Normally I make buying trips to New York once a month and select my gems there," he explained. "But it happens I want to show a special selection to a wealthy client out in Dorset Hills tomorrow. The New York firm was expecting a new shipment from South Africa today, so they promised to make up a parcel and rush it down here tonight."

"How was the messenger travelling?" Collig inquired.

"By train—at least they told me he'd get in on the eight-fifteen."

Collig picked up the phone and called New York City Police Headquarters and asked them to watch the incoming trains. He also called Bayport Headquarters and told his desk sergeant to put out a state-wide alarm for the messenger. Finally he tried to contact the diamond importers, but evidently their office was closed for the night.

"Well, that's about all we can do now," Collig said, hanging up. "But we'll have that messenger here with some answers tomorrow morning or my name's not Clint Collig!"

Frank and Joe hurried home, intending to radio their father immediately and report the mystery. But their mother, who had returned with Aunt Gertrude, told them he could not be contacted.

"Your father called while you boys were gone," she explained. "He and Sam Radley had to rush down to Gary, Indiana, to follow up some urgent clue, and they probably won't get back to Chicago before tomorrow afternoon."

Next morning, the Hardys still had no further word from Jack Wayne, so they drove to the airport to make inquiries about him. At the office of the Ace Air Service, they found a young free-lance pilot named

Tom Lester, who often handled charter flying assignments for Jack.

"Are you boys looking for Jack, too?" he asked.

"We certainly are," Frank replied. He told Tom about the puzzling interrupted radio message.

Tom could offer no explanation. "It certainly sounds strange. What worries me is that Jack filed no flight plan. Ordinarily, under those circumstances, I would have expected him to be back last night."

"Do you think he may have crashed?" Frank inquired anxiously.

"It's possible—especially if his radio conked out. That would explain why he hasn't called for help." Tom rubbed his jaw thoughtfully. "I don't suppose you boys feel like telling me any more about this case you're working on?"

Knowing the young pilot could be trusted, the Hardys told him about the mystery. Tom Lester's keen blue eyes showed interest at once.

"Sounds to me as if Jack's on to something big," Tom surmised. "Maybe he even managed to worm himself into Hirff's confidence. If he went to meet some of the gang, maybe he just hasn't had a chance to contact you again."

"That makes sense, all right," Joe said.

"He didn't leave any message for you on his desk?" Frank asked Lester.

The pilot shook his head. "I didn't notice anything. Let's take another look."

Almost at once Frank pounced on Jack Wayne's phone pad. "Look at this!" he exclaimed.

The pad bore a scribbled notation in Jack's handwriting: *Amethyst calling Seacat.*

Tom read the message with a frown. "That word 'amethyst' ties in with his radio call!"

"Do you know this chap Al Hirff?" Frank asked.

"I know *of* him, and I've seen him," Lester replied, "but I've never met him."

"Let's look for him," Frank suggested. "If we could work him into a casual conversation, we might fish out a clue."

The private rented hangar in which Al Hirff kept his own plane was locked. The Hardys and Tom Lester wandered around the airport, looking into other hangars and the passenger terminal, but could not find Hirff. When Frank and Joe finally left, Tom promised to keep his eyes open for the pilot.

From the airport, the boys drove straight to Bayport Police Headquarters for news of the previous night's diamond mystery. On the way they discussed the curious notation on Jack's phone pad.

"That word 'Seacat' sounds to me like the name of a boat," Joe speculated.

Frank agreed. "You know, Joe, it might even be the name of that mystery cabin cruiser!"

At headquarters the desk sergeant told them to go on into Chief Collig's office. A red-haired man, freckled, and with a wart on one cheek, was seated in front of the chief's desk.

"Glad you're here, boys" Collig told them. "This is Dan O'Bannion, the messenger."

The Hardys listened to O'Bannion's story.

"Like I told Chief Collig," the messenger said, "I took that parcel of gems straight up to Tiffman's office. I delivered them to him and went right back to New York on the next train."

"Did you get a receipt?" Frank asked.

"You bet I did! It's on the chief's desk."

Collig held up an official receipt form. It was signed "Paul Tiffman."

"I've called Tiffman and asked him to come over here," Collig added.

When the diamond merchant arrived, O'Bannion looked astonished. "This isn't the man I gave the gems to!" he exclaimed.

"And I've never seen *you* before, either," Tiffman said tartly.

"You certainly weren't in the office when I arrived," the messenger agreed.

"I was in my office every minute of the evening. And nobody could have taken my place!"

Tiffman added that the signature on the receipt form was not his, and proved it by displaying his driver's licence and other identification cards. O'Bannion shrugged, tight-lipped.

Frank suggested they all go to the Haley Building. "If we reconstruct what happened last night, it may throw a new light on the mystery."

"Good idea, Frank!" Chief Collig said.

In ten minutes they were on their way to Tiffman's office. As they stepped off the lift, the messenger's expression changed.

"What's the matter?" Joe asked him.

O'Bannion pointed to a large, unsightly crack in the wall plaster. "I'm positive that crack wasn't there last night," he said.

"It's been there for the past two weeks," Tiffman said. "Some careless workmen banged into the wall when they were delivering furniture."

When they entered Tiffman's office, O'Bannion looked more bewildered. "This wasn't the office I came to!" he exclaimed. "The furnishings were altogether different!"

"Maybe you need glasses!" Collig snapped. "Didn't you look at the sign on the door?"

"I did look!" O'Bannion flared back. "The office number was 507 and the sign said, 'Paul Tiffman, Gemologist'!"

Chief Collig's face took on a tinge of purple. "I'm sending for the county polygraph expert!" he roared, thumping his fist on the desk. "You and Mr Tiffman and the night watchman are all going to get lie-detector tests!"

"That suits me fine!" O'Bannion snapped.

Frank and Joe were mystified as they drove away from the Haley Building. Both boys would have liked to go out in their boat to sift through their thoughts in the fresh salt air and sunshine. Since the *Sleuth* was not yet repaired, they settled for a drive to the harbour.

The *Napoli* was moored at the dock. Tony was touching up worn spots with varnish, while Chet Morton lolled on a thwart, practising knots. Frank and Joe strolled out to chat with them.

"Anything new on the case?" Tony asked.

"Plenty," Joe grumbled. "The problem is how to unravel it all."

"Rats!" Chet muttered. "I just can't seem to tie a bowline on a bight!"

Suddenly Frank let out a gasp. "Maybe that's what Jack Wayne's message meant!"

·13·

Snoop Camera

Joe gave his brother a puzzled look, at first seeing no connection between Chet's remark and Jack Wayne's interrupted radio message.

"What do you mean, Frank?"

"Look! We've been assuming all along that when Jack said 'tigers bite' he meant the kind of biting that's done with teeth," Frank observed.

Joe exclaimed, "I get it! You think he was talking about the kind of bight spelled b-i-g-h-t!"

"Exactly."

"You mean the message had something to do with a rope or line?" Chet asked blankly.

Frank shook his head. "That wouldn't make much sense. But remember, 'bight' can also mean a sort of bay or indentation in a coastline. In other words, maybe Tigers' Bight is the name of a *place*."

Joe snapped his fingers excitedly. "Sure! Tigers' Bight could be the name of the place Jack was heading for when we saw him fly south!"

"Any of you fellows ever heard that name before?" Frank asked.

Chet shrugged his beefy shoulders. "Not me."

Joe also had to admit that the name was new to him. But Tony frowned thoughtfully. "That rings a bell. I have a hunch I *have* heard it."

"Where?" the Hardys asked in chorus.

"I don't know. But if you're right, it must be some place along the coast. Maybe I've been there in the *Napoli*. Why don't we look at a map?"

Tony opened his boat locker and took out a sailing chart of the Barmet Bay area. He and Chet then climbed up on to the dock, and the boys spread out the chart. But after poring over it for several minutes, they could find no such name as Tigers' Bight.

"Another clue conked out!" Joe muttered.

"Let's not give up too soon," Frank said. "Maybe it's not important enough to show on the map—or maybe the name's not official."

"Why don't you ask old Clams Dagget?" Chet suggested.

"That's an idea," Joe said. "He'd certainly know if anyone would."

Dagget was a retired seafaring man, who now operated a ferry service to Rocky Isle in Barmet Bay.

Frank glanced at his wristwatch. "Clams won't be here to pick up any more passengers before one-thirty. Let's go home and have lunch, Joe. We can stop by later and ask him."

"Okay. I can sure use some grub!"

Each of the boys ate two hamburgers and a generous portion of chips. They were just finishing helpings of Aunt Gertrude's old-fashioned strawberry shortcake when the telephone rang. Tom Lester was calling from the airport.

"Al Hirff has just showed up," the pilot told Frank. "If you want to talk to him, now's your chance."

"Where can we find him?"

"Right now he's in the hangar, checking his plane.

He has a pug nose and wears his hair in long sideburns. You can't miss him."

"Okay. Thanks, Tom." Frank hung up and told Joe. "It's not one o'clock yet. Let's whip out to the airport before we see Clams Dagget."

"Suits me. And say, why don't I take my new camera along and snap Hirff's picture? Dad might recognize him."

"Good idea."

Joe had recently bought an ultraminiature camera from money he had saved. It could be attached to his lapel for taking secret photographs. Both boys slipped on sports jackets to ally suspicion on Joe's manoeuvre.

A short time later they pulled into the airport parking space and headed for Hirff's hangar. The door was open, and inside they could see a big, twin-engined amphibian plane. But the pilot was not in sight.

The boys walked cautiously into the hanger to look around for him. Joe shot an inquisitive glance at the aircraft's cabin, but the fuselage was too high for a full inside view. He climbed up and noticed a folded navigation chart, with pencilled markings, clipped above the pilot's seat.

"Hey, Frank!" Joe exclaimed excitedly. "I see a chart of the Bayport coastal area—and it has some markings on it!"

Frank warned, "Watch it, Joe! Here he comes now!" A man who answered Tom Lester's description of Hirff was striding towards the hangar!

Joe quickly unhooked his lapel camera, held it up, and snapped a picture of the map. Then he jumped down.

Frank met the attack with a judo throw

"What're you louts doing here?" the pilot yelled, charging into the hangar almost at a run.

Joe calmly snapped Hirff's picture, then slipped the camera into the sports jacket pocket. The pilot, livid with rage, tried to hurl Frank aside and get at Joe.

Instead, Frank met the attack. He spun him around with a judo grip and followed with a punch to the jaw that landed the man on the floor. Hirff sat up and blinked in surprise.

Frank repressed a grin. "If you want me to step out of the way, just ask politely."

Hirff got to his feet, scowling. "All right, wise guys! Suppose I call the cops!"

"Go ahead," Frank said coolly. "The hangar was open so we walked in to say hello. Didn't touch a thing."

"When the police get here," Joe added, "maybe we can chat about Tigers' Bight."

The remark was a shot in the dark. Joe had hoped it might startle Hirff or provoke some interesting reaction. But the effect was out of all proportion to what Joe had expected. Hirff's face paled and all the bluster seemed to go out of him.

"I . . . I d-don't know what you're talking about," Hirff faltered. "Sorry if I lost my temper. Thought maybe you kids had sneaked in here to strip the plane or something. Go on now, scram, and we'll forget all about it!"

"Sure, if that's the way you want it." Frank turned to his brother. "Come on," he said.

Joe could not resist a parting taunt. "If you change your mind about calling the police," he needled, "they can find us at the boat dock."

Both boys could feel Al Hirff's eyes burning into

their backs as they walked towards the car park. Driving away, Frank remarked, "Boy! You sure struck gold that time! But I hope it wasn't a mistake, telling him our next move."

Joe shrugged. "I doubt if the gang would try any dirty work in broad daylight. Anyway, if they do, so much the better. That's *one* way to draw 'em into the open!"

At the boat dock a few passengers had already boarded the *Sandpiper*. But Clams Dagget was leaning against a bollard, smoking his corncob pipe, apparently in no hurry to shove off. He greeted the Hardys with a nod. "Hi, lads! How's the detective business?"

"Booming," Frank replied with a smile. "Maybe you can help us. Ever hear of a place called Tigers' Bight?"

"Sure. Down south of the bay. I once lost an anchor there."

The Hardys became excited.

"We couldn't find it on the map," Joe said.

"Ain't surprised," Clams said, without taking the pipe out of his mouth. "That's just a nick-name. 'Bout ten years ago there was a coupl' attacks on swimmers by tiger sharks that come in the bight, so folks thereabouts took to callin' it Tigers' Bight. No one goes there much any more. Pretty desolate now."

Frank took out a pencil and a scrap of paper, and asked Dagget to draw a map so that he and Joe could find the place. The old ferryman obliged.

The Hardys thanked him and started back to their convertible, which they had parked in a vacant parking space on the opposite side of the road. Suddenly Joe let out a startled yelp.

"Frank! Look!" Their car door was open and a

man was raking through the glove compartment!

Frank and Joe started to dart across the road but had to pause for a break in traffic. The man glanced around warily, saw them, and immediately fled through the car park. By the time the Hardys crossed the road, he was leaping into a waiting saloon car. It sped off with a roar.

"Let's go!" Frank shouted, rushing towards the convertible. He slid behind the wheel and Joe slipped in beside him. Frank whirled the car around, sent it bumping and bouncing across the car park, then shot out on to the road.

The chase continued for over a mile, with the saloon clearly in view. Then the Hardys saw it turn off to the right.

Moments later, the convertible reached the same spot and Frank swung the wheel. The car took the turn with a screech of rubber. They were now in a winding country lane with woods on both sides, and the other car was out of sight.

Bang! The convertible suddenly spun out of control. Frank jammed on the brakes, see-sawed the wheel, and managed to bring it to a lurching stop just before it crashed into the trees.

"Whew!" Joe let out a gasp of relief.

Somewhat pale and shaken, the boys climbed out to survey the damage.

"Left front tyre's flat," Frank announced.

"And there's what did it." Joe pointed to a wicked-looking array of tacks, bent nails, and broken glass scattered across the lane. "Those crooks must've tossed the stuff out of their car before we turned into the lane."

Disgusted, the Hardys got a jack out of their boot and set about changing the flat tyre.

Suddenly a small object flew spinning from the trees across the lane. It landed near the convertible and sent up a gush of purple smoke!

Frank stiffened in anger. "Look out, Joe!" he warned. "We're being attacked!"

Three men wearing gas masks had burst out of the woods and were charging towards the boys!

14

Tigers' Lair

As THE smoke bomb burst and Frank yelled his warning, Joe was getting the spare wheel out of the boot, his back turned to the lane.

He whirled at Frank's cry and saw the gas-masked men only a few yards away. He struggled to hoist out the spare wheel and hurl it at them, but two of the thugs pounced on him.

Frank rushed to his brother's assistance, clutching the hub spanner. The third man grabbed his arm, twisted the spanner away from him, and knocked Frank sprawling in the ditch.

In moments, purple smoke blanketed the area. The Hardys gasped and their eyes watered.

Joe's assailants overpowered and searched him, one yanking the lapel camera from his pocket.

Frank was vainly trying to scramble to his feet, but every attempt met with a kick or blow that sent him toppling again. Then, as suddenly as they had appeared, the gas-masked thugs darted away through the smoke.

Joe picked himself up, clawed out a handkerchief to hold over his eyes and nose, and groped his way towards his brother. Frank met him, and hand in hand they ran from the smoke-filled area. In the distance they heard a car start and drive off.

Frank and Joe finally reached clear air. Coughing, the boys slumped against a tree and looked at each other through swollen, red-rimmed eyes.

"Wow! We fell into a trap that time, Frank!"

"Sure did. Joe, we ought to get back to the car and radio the police."

"Okay, but let's wait till the smoke clears."

Presently they were able to return to the convertible. Frank warmed up the short-wave radio and gave the police a description of the saloon car.

Joe, meanwhile, was putting on the spare. "Sorry I got us into this, Frank," he apologized. "I shouldn't have said anything to Hirff about Tigers' Bight."

"Never mind. They still wouldn't have nailed us if we'd used our heads."

"How do you figure that?"

"That guy rifling our glove compartment was probably a decoy," Frank reasoned. "If he didn't find what he was after, I'll bet his orders were to let us spot him. They knew we'd go after him, so they had the tyre-puncture trick and the gas attack all set up beforehand."

Joe shook his head ruefully. "Boy! Now I *really* feel like a chump!"

"Did they get your camera?"

"Yes. I'm glad it was insured!" Joe grinned. "But there's one thing they *didn't* get."

"What's that?"

"Take a look in the glove compartment."

Frank did so, then turned in astonishment. "The film! How did that get in there?"

"Simple. I unloaded the camera while we were driving after 'em." Joe chuckled as he wrestled the spare wheel into the boot. "I had a hunch there might be trouble if we caught up with those characters—and the glove compartment looked safe because it had already been searched."

"Nice going, Joe!"

As they were driving home, Joe remarked, "Hirff called the signals on that attack."

"Sure, but try and prove it. He probably phoned his pals the second we left the airport and has a nice, clear-cut alibi for himself."

As soon as they arrived home, the boys developed the film and made an enlarged print of the chart. As expected, it showed the Bayport coastal area. A notch in the coastline south of Barmet Bay had been circled in pencil.

"It's the place on Clams Dagget's map—Tigers' Bight!" Frank exclaimed, then frowned. "I don't get it, Joe. Hirff knew we'd heard about Tigers' Bight, and we were bound to locate it. So why was he so eager to get the film back?"

"You're overlooking something, Frank—right here." Joe pointed to an X mark near the bight, barely visible on the print.

Frank gave a whistle. "Wonder what's there!"

"Maybe enough evidence to put the gang behind bars," Joe surmised. "This photo would link them to whatever that X stands for."

"Wow!" Frank was jubilant. "I have a feeling we're really getting somewhere now, Joe!"

"If only we knew what those words on Jack's phone pad meant—'Amethyst calling Seacat.' "

"Sounds like a radio call," Frank mused. "It would tie in with our guess about 'Seacat.' "

"In other words, a radio call to a boat."

"Right. But the 'Amethyst' part stumps me—unless that's the name of another boat—or maybe of a plane that's doing the calling."

"That's it, Frank!" Joe snapped his fingers excitedly. "It could be a code name for Jack's own plane—or even for Jack himself!"

"Right. Let's assume Tom Lester's hunch is correct—that Jack managed to worm his way into Hirff's gang. And let's assume *your* hunch is correct that he was flying to Tigers' Bight."

"Okay. So what then?" Joe asked.

"Don't you see? Maybe Jack was flying there on Hirff's instructions. Hirff told him to contact a boat named the *Seacat* by radio and then rendezvous with it in Tigers' Bight!"

"Perfect!" Joe exclaimed. "Frank, if Jack was flying a mission for the gang, that radio message wasn't sabotaged. It must have been interrupted accidentally."

"I'll check right now!" Frank said. He called the Bayport radio station and learned that it, too, had experienced freakish transmission difficulties the day before—apparently due to sunspots.

"Frank, let's go to Tigers' Bight and find out what that X stands for," Joe proposed. "While we're at it, we may spot Jack's plane!"

"Okay," Frank agreed. "But let's call Dad first. He may be back at the hotel by now."

The boys were able to contact Fenton Hardy. "How'd you make out in Gary, Dad?" Frank asked.

"We ran into a blank wall," the detective replied. "The getaway car was traced there. But I'm sure now it was just a false scent to make us think the thieves had fled to that area to hide out."

When Mr Hardy heard about the Haley Building mystery and the vanished diamonds, he concluded that the same jewel thieves had struck again.

"Sam and I had better fly back there as soon as possible," he told Frank. "We'll try to be in Bayport some time tonight..'

Mr Hardy listened with keen interest to Frank's report about Al Hirff, the notation on Jack's phone pad, the gas-bomb attack on the boys, and their theory about Tigers' Bight.

After concluding the conversation, the boys drove to Bayport harbour. They rented a motor boat and started into the bay. As they passed the jetty, they sighted the *Napoli*, with Tony and Chet aboard.

The boys hailed one another, and brought their boats alongside. Frank told them where he and his brother were heading.

"Why pay rent on that job?" Tony exclaimed eagerly. "I'll take you there in the *Napoli!*"

Frank considered a moment, then shook his head. "There's another job you can do."

"Name it."

"We have a hunch that 'Seacat' may be the name of the gang's cabin cruiser," Frank explained. "How about cruising all the coves around here and see if you can spot a boat by that name?"

Tony and Chet agreed, and the Hardys resumed their course. Reaching the mouth of Barmet Bay, they headed southward along the coast. After half an hour's run they sighted Tigers' Bight.

"If Tigers' Bight is just a local nickname, I

wonder how the gang picked it up," Joe mused.

"They must have heard it from some local boatman or fisherman," Frank reasoned.

Joe slowed the motor as they cruised into the bight. The cove was wooded on all sides, with a strip of flat sandy beach extending for about a quarter of a mile. The rest of the shore was rocky.

"Frank, that beach would have made a good landing strip for *Skyhappy Sal*," Joe suggested. "What say we take a look for plane tracks?"

"Good idea."

Joe brought the motor boat in close and anchored. The boys pulled off their shoes and socks and waded ashore. The sand appeared unmarked.

"You could still be right," Frank told his brother. "The tracks may have been washed out during high tide."

Returning to their boat, the Hardys consulted their photographic blow-up of Hirff's chart. The X mark lay inland from the bight on a narrow creek which flowed not far from the beach. Apart from a few gulls screeching overhead and the noise of the surf outside the bight, the area was calm and silent.

Frank frowned at the racket of the motor as Joe steered towards the creek. "If any of the gang's around here, we certainly won't take 'em by surprise," he remarked.

Joe nosed the boat gently into the creek. Frank moored it to a rock and they headed inland on foot. The brothers had hiked only a short distance along the winding stream when they sighted a dilapidated cabin nestled among trees.

"So that's what the X mark stood for!" Joe exclaimed.

The boys advanced cautiously to reconnoitre the cabin. Suddenly they were startled by the sound of an aircraft engine revving up along the bight. A moment later the plane soared into view among the trees.

"It's *Skyhappy Sal!*" Frank yelled.

The craft was heading seaward. To the boys' astonishment it banked and circled sharply, then came swooping in low—straight towards them! The pilot cut the engine, and the Hardys caught a fleeting glimpse of Jack Wayne and another man in the plane's cabin. Jack waved to them frantically.

"Don't go into that cabin!" he shouted.

The pilot opened up the engine, trying to work up flying speed again—but the plane dipped and went into a stall.

"He's going to crack up!" Joe yelled.

An instant later the boys heard a terrific impact and the crash of crumbling metal!

15

Puzzling Reports

FEARING the worst, Frank and Joe ran along the creek bank. As they emerged from the trees, they saw that the plane had hit the beach about two hundred yards away. Its tail was high in the air and one wing had crumpled.

The Hardys ran towards the crashed aircraft. Jack was evidently still in the plane, but his companion had been hurled from the cabin by the force of the impact. He was getting dazedly to his feet and brushing off the sand that smeared him from head to foot. At the sight of the boys, the man began groping frantically on the ground.

"He may be hunting for his gun!" Frank warned. "We'd better nail him fast!"

Frank's guess seemed to be correct, for as the Hardys closed in, the man gave up his search and fled into the woods. Joe would have chased him, but Frank grabbed his brother's arm and pointed to *Skyhappy Sal*. Flames were licking the fuselage!

"Never mind that guy! Help me get Jack out!"

The right side of the plane, from which the gunman had been thrown, was uppermost. The door was hanging wide open. Frank climbed inside, heedless of the sizzling flames. Jack lay wedged behind the control column, bleeding and motionless.

"He risked his life to warn us!" Frank thought. "I sure hope he's still alive!"

There was no time to be gentle. Frank manoeuvred the limp form out as best he could. Legs first, Jack was passed through the cabin doorway. Both the Hardys were streaming with perspiration as they lurched away from the plane, lugging the pilot between them.

At a safe distance from the wrecked aircraft, they laid Jack down on the sand and turned back to stare at *Skyhappy Sal*. The blaze was now crackling furiously.

"Some of the electrical gear must have shorted," Joe said.

"We'll never know," Frank muttered. "Once the fuel tank blows, she'll—"

His words were cut short as the plane exploded into a ball of fire. A column of smoke and flame shot high in the air.

"Wow! We made it just in time!" Joe gasped in a shaky voice.

The boys turned their attention to Jack Wayne. His face and shirt were streaked with blood from a scalp wound. Frank felt the pilot's pulse and knelt to listen for a heartbeat.

"Thank goodness! He's still alive!" Frank reported tensely.

Joe ripped off a piece of his own shirt-tail to make a bandage. Fortunately, although the pilot's hair was matted with blood from the wound, active bleeding appeared to have ceased.

Frank wiped Jack's face with a scrap of cloth moistened with water. Presently the pilot stirred and opened his eyes. As he saw Frank and Joe bending over him, his lips twitched into a smile of relief.

"Sure glad you boys are safe," he murmured.

"Glad *we're* safe!" Joe echoed. He flashed his brother a puzzled glance.

"Must have something to do with the cabin," Frank said. "You were trying to warn us—is that it, Jack?"

Their friend gave a faint nod. "I was waiting there with that other guy . . . to meet the boss. Then he . . . he got word by radio that you two might show up. Radio message said to booby-trap the cabin w-with explosive . . . and pull out."

"Wait, let's get this straight," Frank put in hastily. "You flew here because Hirff offered you a chance to join the gang?"

Again the pilot nodded.

"And your plane was hidden in the brush so no one would spot it?" Joe added.

"Th-that's right," Jack mumbled. "We were just about to leave when your boat pulled in. Barney, he's the fellow who was with me . . . he said we should lie low till you were out of sight . . . then take off . . ."

Jack's voice was getting weaker. Frank urged him not to talk, but the pilot, now lapsing back into unconsciousness, seemed not to hear.

"B-Barney was holding a gun on me . . . testing me to s-see what I'd do. Only way I could warn you was to——"

Suddenly Jack's head lolled to one side.

"He's passed out again, poor guy," Frank said, checking the pilot's pulse.

"He saved our lives, Frank," Joe murmured. "With that cabin deserted, we'd have walked inside and been blown sky-high if Jack hadn't—"

The wilderness quiet was suddenly shattered by the

staccato noise of a boat engine. The Hardys leaped to their feet and saw their own motor boat shoot out from the creek! Aboard was the man who had been hurled clear of the plane—the man whom Jack had called Barney.

"What a couple of nitwits we are!" Joe burst out furiously. "While we were talking here, we let him circle through the woods and grab our boat!"

There was no possible chance of retrieving the craft. It was already picking up speed—heading out of the bight towards the open sea.

"The prize boner of all time!" Frank groaned. "We're stranded here, Joe! And Jack needs medical attention!"

The photographic print of the map was in the boat, and neither boy could remember any inland details, but Joe felt sure the nearest road was at least ten miles away.

"Looks as though we have two choices, Joe," Frank said thoughtfully. "We can wait here till the folks back in Bayport get worried and come looking for us. Or one of us can try to find a road and flag down a car for help."

Joe shook his head. "Pretty long shot. Whoever went might not be able to find his way through the woods before dark. But there's one other possibility, Frank."

"Such as?"

"Try to get into the cabin without exploding the booby trap and use the gang's radio."

"You're right! I never thought of that." Frank rubbed his jaw worriedly and considered.

The boys' debate was cut short as they saw a small cruiser heading into the bight. Frank and Joe jumped up and down, yelling and waving their arms, but they soon realized the signals were unnecessary. The cruiser evidently had been attracted to the scene by the smoke and flame of the burning aircraft.

The skipper of the cruiser brought his craft in close to the boys and shouted through cupped hands, "What happened? Do you need help?"

"We sure do!" Frank yelled back. "A plane crashed and the pilot's injured! We're stranded here! Can you get us to Bayport?"

"You bet I will!" the skipper replied heartily.

Normally the Hardys would not have risked moving a man in Jack's condition. But they felt they had no choice. Using a tarpaulin from the cruiser as a make-shift stretcher, they carried him through the shallow water and loaded him gently aboard the boat.

Mr Webb, the elderly, white-haired owner of the cruiser, revved his engine and they started out of the bight.

"Too bad I have no radio, boys, or we could call ahead and have an ambulance waiting."

"We're mighty grateful, anyhow, sir," Frank replied. "If you hadn't come along, I don't know what we would have done."

There seemed little chance of sighting or overtaking the stolen motor boat. But as they approached the bay, Joe thought he glimpsed the craft and asked to borrow Mr Webb's binoculars.

"That's our boy, all right!" he said a moment later, passing the glasses to Frank. "He's heading somewhere near Sea Gull Cove!"

Minutes after they docked, an ambulance came screeching to the scene in response to a phone call by Frank. A doctor gave Jack emergency treatment. Then the injured pilot was transferred from the boat on a stretcher. The Hardys followed in their convertible as the ambulance sped off, siren wailing.

From the hospital, Frank telephoned Police Chief Collig and made a full report. The chief promised to have state troopers dispatched at once to the cabin to disarm the booby trap and search for clues. He also promised an immediate search for the stolen boat.

"Incidentally, Frank," Collig went on, "Tiffman, the messenger, and the watchman were all given lie-detector tests this afternoon."

"How'd they make out?" Frank asked.

"Believe it or not, all three are in the clear." Collig sounded thoroughly irritated and baffled. "I don't know what kind of trick was played, but I'll get to the bottom of this yet!"

After hanging up, Frank called the boat hire firm and explained what had happened. "I'm sure the police will recover it," he added.

A few minutes later a doctor stepped out of the emergency ward. "Your friend seems to be in fair shape—no broken bones," he told the boys. "However, he's still unconscious and may have a concussion." The Hardys felt relieved that the news was no worse.

It was now past six o'clock, and the boys were due home for dinner. But Frank had an idea which he urgently wanted to check out with Mike, the night watchman at the Haley Buildings. He telephoned home, then the brothers drove from the hospital.

"What can I do for you, boys?" Mike greeted them. "Still huntin' clues to what happened here last night?"

"Well, sort of," Frank said. "I'd like to ask you some questions and find out exactly what took place before and after the messenger came."

"Okay, shoot!"

Probing insistently, Frank had the watchman go over everything that had happened the night before. It turned out that Mike's recollection was hazy for two periods of about twenty minutes each—one around seven o'clock and the other around eight-forty-five.

"Guess I must've dozed off," the watchman admitted a bit shamefacedly. "I remember comin' to with a start both times."

As the boys left the building and got into their car, Joe remarked, "So he blacked out twice! That sounds like the same method used on all the other jewel robberies!"

"Which backs up Dad's hunch." Frank's voice was tense. "Joe, I think I can explain the mystery of what happened here last night!"

·16·

Riddle with Three Answers

Joe glanced eagerly at his brother as their convertible pulled away from the kerb. "Let's hear your theory, Frank!"

"Chief Collig says the lie-detector tests show that all three people involved are telling the truth," Frank began. "The watchman, the messenger, and Mr Tiffman."

"So?"

"Therefore," Frank continued, "we can assume the watchman did take the messenger up in the lift—but not to the fifth floor. And O'Bannion did deliver the gems—but not to Tiffman's office."

"Now wait a minute," Joe said. "If O'Bannion didn't take the diamonds to Tiffman's office, where did he take them?"

"To an office on the sixth floor—or possibly the fourth."

"How do you figure that?"

"The watchman blacked out twice," Frank replied. "During that time, someone could have tampered with the lift controls and also with the office numbers."

Joe frowned. "So Mike *thought* he was letting the messenger off on five. But actually it was one floor higher or lower."

"Right."

"Could the lift controls actually be doctored to fool the operator that way?" Joe asked.

Frank nodded as he braked for a red light. "I'm sure they could, Joe. That lift is a push-button job with solid doors—not an old-fashioned cage with manual control. A smart mechanic could make the lift stop at the *wrong* floor just by switching a few wires beforehand—and the person inside wouldn't know the difference—even the watchman himself—unless he timed the ride."

"How about when the messenger rang to go down?" Joe asked.

"That makes a light flash on the control panel," Frank replied. "But let's say the wiring had been tampered with. O'Bannion rings from Six, but the light shows Five. Mike pushes the button for Five—but the elevator actually goes up to Six, where O'Bannion is waiting. Neither one realizes anything is wrong."

"Wow! Pretty slick!" Joe exclaimed. "And the office numbers were switched too, eh?"

"Yes—probably by a confederate, to speed up the job. The doors aren't glazed, with the numbers and names painted on them. They have metal numerals and name plates screwed on."

"Which would be easy to change," Joe agreed. "The crooks could have had duplicate name plates made up beforehand to match the ones on Five."

"And they wouldn't have needed to substitute all of them," Frank added as he swung off Main Street into the residential area of Bayport. "Just on the doors the messenger would see. And, of course, substitute fives for the sixes."

"Sounds foolproof," Joe said. "One of the crooks waits in the phoney office and takes the gems. Then after the messenger leaves, they black out the watchman again and switch everything back the way it was before."

"Right," Frank replied. "Now the question is—how do the crooks do their blackout trick?"

"I've been thinking about that," Joe brooded. "Frank, that may be where Professor Darrow and his scientific know-how come into the picture."

"You mean he's in cahoots with Strang?"

"Maybe." Joe shrugged. "Perhaps he's even trying to work off a grudge against society because no one would back his research, or he may have been brainwashed."

"Could be," Frank agreed. "He sounded a bit odd from what Dean Gibbs told us."

Frank swung into the Hardys' drive. "Another thing, Joe—what did that remark you heard on the tunnel phone mean?"

"About the 'disappearing floor'? I have a hunch it referred to the Haley Building job."

"That's one possibility. Actually, there are *three* 'disappearing floors.' One—that phonily numbered floor at the Haley Building. Two—the hinged tiled summerhouse floor. And three—that invisible floor of Old Man Perth's bedroom-study at the mansion."

Joe chuckled. "A riddle with three answers!"

Aunt Gertrude suddenly thrust her head out of the side door. "Are you expecting dinner to be served in the car? Food's cold already!"

"Sorry, Aunty," Frank said. "It's my fault."

Miss Hardy was curious about the latest developments in the case. At the table she listened eagerly as the boys told about the startling events at Tigers' Bight. Both she and Mrs Hardy expressed concern over Jack Wayne.

"Oh, I hope there won't be any after-effects," said the boys' mother.

Before the brothers could be served dessert, Tony and Chet arrived with more exciting news.

"We found a cruiser called the *Seacat!*" Tony announced breathlessly. "It looks like the one we saw before that frogman attacked Joe!"

"Where is it now?" Frank asked.

"In one of those coves just off Shore Road," Chet blurted out.

Aunt Gertrude spluttered indignantly as Frank and Joe hurried away without waiting for any dessert. They jumped into their convertible and set off after Chet's jalopy.

Dusk was falling as the four friends pulled up near the cove. An old, rather battered-looking coupé was parked among the trees.

"Must belong to someone on the cruiser," Tony speculated. "There's nothing else around here."

"I have an idea," Joe said. "Let me take the convertible, Frank. Chet, you park in that next grove, and I'll meet you fellows in a few minutes down in that clump of willows on the cove."

The others agreed, wondering what he had in mind. After Joe had made a U-turn and driven off, Chet parked his own car, then started down the hillside towards the cove with Frank and Tony.

The three boys hid among the willows and looked out across the water. The cruiser lay silently at anchor amid the deepening twilight, with a dinghy tied alongside. A faint, wavering light came through the cabin portholes.

Ten minutes went by. At last Joe joined them.

"I borrowed Dad's radio signal-sender," he explained, "and attached it to the axle of that coupé so we can trail it."

"Smart idea," Frank said approvingly.

A few more minutes passed. Then the light aboard the cruiser went out. Presently a shadowy figure emerged from the cabin, but it was now too dark for the boys to make out the man's features. He glanced around furtively, then climbed into the dinghy and began rowing ashore.

"He certainly acted sneaky," Tony whispered.

"He's probably not the owner," Frank surmised. "I'll bet he had no right to be aboard."

The man rowed across the cove, moored the dinghy to a tree, and started up the hillside.

"He must be the person who parked that coupé," Joe muttered excitedly.

The boys hurried back to their own cars. Joe had parked in the grove, close to Chet's jalopy. Almost instantly they heard the coupé start up, and a moment later it drove past. Joe switched on the special receiver for the radio-tailing device. A low, steady whirring wail issued from the speaker.

"Okay, let's go!" he told Frank.

The convertible swung out on to the road. Chet's jalopy followed. Frank kept his headlights dimmed and stayed a safe distance behind the coupé. It circled Bayport and turned on to the road the black sports car had taken three nights earlier. Joe traced the coupé's course by manipulating a loop antenna.

"He's going to the Perth mansion!" Joe exclaimed as a sudden fade in the radio howl announced a turn by their quarry.

The boys pulled off the road and waited a few minutes so as not to betray themselves. Then they, too, entered the rough lane. After parking in some shrubbery, they began searching for the coupé. Frank soon spotted it standing half-hidden among some trees farther down the lane.

"Looks as though he's trying to stay undercover himself," Tony muttered.

"I'm sure he's not one of Strang's men," Frank agreed as Joe jotted down the licence number.

"How are we going to find him?" Chet asked.

"Scout around and use your eyes," Joe replied.

The four boys started up the slope. They all swung around with a start as a bloodthirsty snarl sent their pulse rates skyrocketing. Frank had to clamp a hand over Chet's mouth to prevent the stout youth from shrieking.

"Steady, pal! That's just a mechanical spook hound —to scare people like us."

Chet gulped as the fiery-eyed hound snarled again.

"It just succeeded with one person!" the fat boy announced and started back down the slope. Frank calmed him and they went on. Tony and Chet waited in the shadows as Frank and Joe made their way to the house. They had just reached the porch when they heard a muffled "Ssst!" from Tony and turned.

A white phantom was moving towards the house.

"The galloping ghost!" Joe gasped.

The boys went racing towards it, but the ghostly figure detected their approach and fled.

"That ghost must have eyes in the back of his head!" Joe muttered angrily, still running.

The spectre soon disappeared from view among the trees. Frank acted on a hunch. He short-cut back to the coupé and hid among some bushes. A white figure suddenly loomed out of the darkness. It headed straight for the car and yanked open the door. Before the phantom could climb inside, Frank pounced on him!

The spook-masquerader battled wildly, but the three other boys quickly arrived on the scene and helped Frank pin him against the car.

"Pretty solid for a ghost!" Chet remarked.

"Not as solid as you," Joe quipped. "But there's flesh under that spook costume!"

"Let's have a look at him," Frank added, and pulled off the prowler's hood.

· 17 ·

The Second Spectre

CHET let out a gasp of surprise as Tony shone a torch on the man's face. "It's that creep we picked up unconscious the other night!"

"And also the thief who stole Iola and Callie's amethyst," Frank added.

The man cowered in the glare of Tony's beam. "Please, boys," he whined, "I meant no harm. This ghost masquerade was just intended as a hoax. Nothing more than a joke."

"Some joke," Tony said dryly.

"How about stealing that amethyst?" Chet growled. "That was a joke too?"

The man's face turned pale. "No, it—it was wrong of me, tricking you with that oil fire and snatching the stone right out of your house." He wet his lips nervously. "But I had to have it! By rights, the stone belongs to me."

The boys were puzzled.

"How does it 'belong' to you?" Joe asked.

The man squirmed uncomfortably. "It doesn't matter," he mumbled. "You'll find what you're after in my right-hand coat pocket."

Joe reached inside the white robe. A moment later his hand emerged holding a purple stone.

"The amethyst!" Chet exclaimed. Joe turned it over to him to give back to the girls.

"You still haven't answered my brother's question," Frank said in a cold voice. "Why did you say the amethyst belonged to you?"

The prisoner had an angry look, like that of a trapped animal. "I told you it doesn't matter!" he retorted. "I know what you boys are up to! You're trying to worm information out of me, hoping you can get all the stones for yourselves!"

"Now listen," Frank snapped, "I don't know what you mean by that remark, but you'd better talk fast or we'll call the police! I think we should, anyway."

"No, no! Please!" The prisoner seemed to crumble. "I can't afford to go to jail now—there's so much to do! I can explain. I'll tell you whatever you want to know."

"You can begin by answering Joe's question—and then tell us why you've been prowling around in that spook get-up."

"All right." The man gulped and tried to pull himself together. "My name is Karl Nyland Jr. Years ago, my father discovered an amethyst lode somewhere near Bayport. He went to old Jerome Perth for financial backing—they even signed a partnership agreement. But that swindler, Perth, double-crossed him!"

"How so?" Frank asked.

"Perth bought the site in his own name, then kept stalling my father off—said he was waiting for a geologist's report. Finally my father got fed up. They quarrelled and Perth had my father thrown out of the mansion. But first Perth taunted him. He said the partnership papers, and some amethysts my father had brought him, were kept in a place outside the mansion where anyone could get at them—but my father wouldn't be smart enough to find it."

"Boy! Sounds as if Perth was a real snake-in-the-grass!" Tony muttered.

"That man was evil," Nyland declared, "but he got his just desserts. The quarrel brought on a heart attack and he died the next day."

"Didn't the partnership papers turn up when the old man's estate was settled?" Frank asked.

"No, his lawyers claimed that no such papers, nor the amethysts, were among Perth's effects. My father kept searching secretly for a long time after that, but he never could find the hiding place."

Joe snapped his fingers. "He must have been the ghostly figure that people thought was haunting this place!"

"Yes, he was searching here the night the nephew died," Nyland admitted. "That's what gave him the idea of dressing as a ghost. He thought it might help to scare tenants away and keep the mansion unoccupied until he could locate the secret cache. But he never found it."

"At least his scheme to scare people away worked," Chet put in. "And now you've been trying the same stunt?"

Nyland nodded guiltily. "I received a bad electrical shock when I was searching here the other night. That's when you boys found me unconscious. Since you'd seen my face, I decided I'd better use a ghost costume as a disguise, in case you came back to look for me."

"How come you waited so long to begin searching?" Joe inquired.

"I was a child living with relatives in another state

when Perth swindled my father," Nyland explained. "It was only recently that I ran across my father's diary and read the whole story. My wife's been very ill, and I was in debt from the hospital bills—so I decided to come to Bayport and try to find the lode and the partnership papers."

"Sounds like a wild-goose chase," Frank said.

The man nodded. "That's just what it's been. All I have to show are these." The man reached into his pocket and pulled out a dozen small metal discs. Each bore a picture of a violet above a dragon's head!

"Perth's lucky pieces!" Joe exclaimed. "We found one near the mansion—you must have dropped it there!"

"Could be," Nyland admitted.

"Do you know what the design was supposed to signify?" Frank asked.

"Not really," Nyland said, then added ruefully, "To me, the dragon is Perth—and the violet's a symbol of the lovely purple stones he tricked my father out of."

Joe frowned. "Was there only one copy of the partnership agreement?"

"Exactly. Perth was sly about that. My father foolishly trusted him and didn't insist on two copies being drawn up."

"Then why wouldn't Perth simply destroy the agreement when the deed was in his name?"

"He was using it to soft-soap my father and keep him quiet—also to keep him on a string. You see, my father had made two earlier gem strikes for a mining company. Perth no doubt hoped he might make other valuable finds. And I'm sure Perth was cruel enough to keep the agreement after their quarrel—just to tantalize and torment my father."

"You have no idea where the amethyst lode was located?" Joe asked.

Nyland shook his head dejectedly. "No, Perth owned a great deal of property, but it was all sold off after his death. And the diary didn't say. That's why I shadowed those two girls after I overheard them telling the gem-shop proprietor about finding a large amethyst. I hoped they might lead me to the lode."

"What were you doing aboard that cruiser tonight?" Tony inquired.

Nyland shrugged. "Just a hunch. There's something strange about those people living at the mansion now. This afternoon I saw two of them in town and heard them mention the word 'amethyst.' I thought maybe they had found the papers relating to the lode, so I shadowed one of them. He went to that boat, and after he left I climbed aboard myself. But it was a waste of time—I found nothing."

Nyland's shoulders sagged. Half sobbing, he began to tell the boys about his wife's illness and the debts that had made him desperate. He pleaded with them not to turn him over to the police. The Hardys, Chet, and Tony felt perplexed and embarrassed. They decided to leave the decision to Mr Hardy.

Suddenly a light went on in an upstairs window of the mansion. Joe exclaimed, "It's the window where we spotted that man who looked like Professor Darrow! Frank, let's stay here—we may see him again!"

Frank glanced at Chet and Tony. "Dad's due in tonight. Would you two take Nyland to our house and keep him there till Dad arrives?"

"Sure. I can call my folks," Tony replied.

"Same here. And maybe your Aunt Gertrude will make us all a snack," Chet said hopefully.

Nyland, anxious to avoid arrest, agreed to accompany them with his hands tied and to make no trouble. All three went off in Chet's car.

"The man's odd, but I think he was telling the truth," Frank said. "He sure sounds as if he's been under a nervous strain."

The Hardys started back up the slope. Cautiously they began making their way through the wooded grounds towards the mansion.

Suddenly there was a weird scream from close by—then another, weaker scream, ending in the same gasped-out words they had heard before:

"*Th-th-the floor!*"

Frank and Joe froze. "It's only a trick," Frank muttered as they started forward again.

They were nearing the house when both boys went cold with shock. *A glowing white figure had risen from the ground!*

"We caught the spook already," Joe whispered.

"It's a fake, Joe. . . . It must be a fake!" Frank stared in horrified fascination.

The thing was moving towards them, flapping!

Resisting an impulse to run, the Hardys closed in. They clutched at the spectre. Joe gave a chuckle of relief as he felt the wire framework underneath. It was covered with some kind of synthetic cloth, which evidently had been dipped in white phosphorescent dye.

"Just a pop-up scarecrow, Frank! We must have stepped on the release mechanism back there."

"Right, Joe. And look at the wheels. The breeze blew it towards us!"

They went on. In the shadow of a tree they paused and looked up at the lighted window. Shelves with bottles and test tubes, and some electrical apparatus, could be seen.

"A laboratory!" Joe murmured.

Behind the shaded windows on the ground floor a radio was blaring dance music.

Suddenly a man moved into view at the upper-floor window. Bald and bespectacled, he was holding an open book in one hand.

"There he is!" Frank whispered.

"That's Darrow, all right," Joe agreed. "If only we could talk to him!"

"Fat chance with Strang and his gang around. Anyway, we've seen all we need to. Let's go home and wait for Dad."

Turning, the brothers started back across the grounds to their car. Halfway down the slope, they heard the screams and the choking voice again.

"Hold it, Joe," Frank hissed. "That tiled floor's around here somewhere. Did you notice that we always hear the screams near here?"

The boys shone their flashlights carefully about the ground. Suddenly Joe's beam disclosed a small metal object sticking up from the grass.

"I'll bet that's it, Frank! Must be some kind of sensor—maybe infra-red—that triggers off a tape-recording when anyone comes near."

Joe moved closer to examine it. Again the voice shrieked! Startled, Joe backed off hastily and his foot struck a rock.

Frank gave a cry of dismay as the ground gave way under his feet. Down he plunged!

134 THE DISAPPEARING FLOOR

"The tunnel exit!" Joe exclaimed. "My foot hit a rock—same thing that happened last night. That must be what opens it from the outside."

"Right. And look at all this turf and brushwood that fell in with me—they *do* camouflage the tiled floor." Frank shone his flashlight into the tunnel. "Wonder if we could get into the house this way, past Strang and his henchmen, and talk to Professor Darrow?"

Joe leaped down beside Frank. "I'm game! Let's find out where the tunnel leads!"

·18·

A Strange Machine

FRANK had been only half serious when he spoke of trying to enter the house through the tunnel. But Joe's excitement communicated itself to him. This might be a chance to get information or a clue that would break the case!

"Okay. Let's take a look."

They started into the tunnel, one behind the other. Frank led the way, probing the darkness with the yellow beam of his flashlight.

"Watch that intercom!" Joe warned. "We don't want another chat with Waxie's pal!"

The brick-walled passageway went on for hundreds of feet. The boys came at last to a door. It had a lock but opened freely when Frank tried the knob. "It must unlock automatically when the tiled floor opens," he whispered.

"In that case, why the intercom?"

Frank shrugged. "Someone might want to hide in the tunnel but still be able to communicate with the house. Or maybe they post a lookout at the tunnel exit sometimes and have him report back by phone."

The boys played their torches around. "We must be in the basement of the mansion," Joe murmured.

The huge, cement-floored area was dank and musty. There was a coal bunker, a grimy-looking, cobwebbed furnace, and an air-conditioning unit that looked brand new. Far at the rear was a flight of stairs leading upwards.

Frank asked his brother, "Should we risk it? Or turn back?"

"Don't be silly! We're going to talk to Professor Darrow, remember?"

The boys walked cautiously towards the stairway and tiptoed up. They found that the first flight ended at the kitchen of the sprawling mansion. From here another flight led upwards. The stairs creaked under the boys' tread, but fortunately the radio music racketing in the ground-floor front rooms covered their noise.

Reaching the upper floor, the boys went along a corridor towards the front of the house. The hallway twisted and turned as if the mansion had been designed with an eccentric floor plan. After passing several doors, the Hardys stopped at one which showed light underneath.

"This must be the laboratory," Frank whispered.

Joe held up crossed fingers. "Okay. Let's find out."

Frank opened the door. Professor Darrow was holding a test tube of coloured liquid up to the light. He turned as the boys entered—and gave such a violent start that the liquid splashed on his workbench!

"Professor Darrow—?" Frank inquired. Joe closed the door softly behind them.

The scientist's hand trembled as he placed the test tube in a rack. He stared at the Hardys through his steel-rimmed glasses and his eyes were full of fear.

"Who are you? What do you want?" he blurted out in a shrill, staccato voice.

The muffled strains of the radio music could be heard through the floor.

Instantly, Frank stiffened and froze

"We're Frank and Joe Hardy, sir," Frank began. "Our father is Fenton Hardy."

He assumed the name would be familiar to a crime-detection expert. But Darrow glared at them, giving no sign of recognition.

"Fenton Hardy—the private investigator," Joe emphasized. "Maybe you've heard of him."

"Maybe." The scientist's eyes bored through the boys. He wore a white lab coat and his wispy fringe of grey hair frothed out wildly around his narrow skull. "Why did you come here?"

"Dean Gibbs of Western State asked us to locate you and—" Frank started to explain.

"He would! You've come here to spy on me!"

"That's not true!" Frank exclaimed.

"The dean wired us on behalf of your sister," Joe put in hastily. "She'd like you to get in touch with her. She's probably worried because she hasn't heard from—"

Joe broke off suddenly as he noticed the professor's hand inching towards a strange device on his work-bench. It looked somewhat like a round, portable electric heater.

"*Look out, Frank!*"

Joe leaped clear in the nick of time as Professor Darrow snatched up the device. But Frank did not react fast enough. A dazzle of light flared from the machine. Instantly Frank stiffened and froze, statue-like.

He had blacked out!

An electric cord ran from the machine to a wall socket. Joe yanked the plug out before Darrow could aim the device at him.

"Help! Help!" the professor shouted.

Joe glanced around frantically. The radio music

from below had stopped. A moment later came the sound of feet pounding up the stairs!

"Strang and his boys!" Joe thought. "I'll have to duck fast! But where?"

Suddenly Darrow lunged at him and tried to pin the boy's arms. Joe wrenched free and gave the professor a hard shove that sent him reeling backwards. Darrow crashed into a corner of the workbench and went down in a cascade of glass tubing, retorts, and other laboratory apparatus.

Like a flash, Joe darted out through a doorway that led to an adjoining room. The door slammed behind him just as Strang and several henchmen came surging into the laboratory.

"That way!" Darrow shrilled, pointing in the direction of Joe's flight. "Through that door!"

The gang rushed through a maze of connecting rooms. Joe, concealed behind the heavy, dark-red curtains in the room next to the lab, could hear Strang barking out orders.

A moment later the master jewel thief strode past Joe's hiding place on his way back to the laboratory. Through the open doorway, Joe heard him talking to the professor.

"Yes, I know the boy. Recognized him at once," came Strang's voice, evidently referring to Frank. "He and his brother are the sons of a clever spy who must have been sent to Bayport purposely to steal your invention.'

"Just what I feared!" Darrow replied. "Then it's not true that they're connected in any way with Fenton Hardy?"

"Certainly not! In fact, Hardy's now on my payroll, working undercover to safeguard your research."

Strang's voice became firm and persuasive. "Don't worry, Professor! My men are bound to catch the other boy. Then we'll hand them both over to the FBI."

"I certainly hope you're right!" Darrow sighed heavily. "First the university authorities and jealous colleagues blocked my research grant at school! And now spies hounding me!"

"By the way," Joe heard Strang ask, "how deeply did you black this kid out?"

"Just a light dose. But it should hold him long enough to—"

A loud alarm bell rang on the ground floor, cutting short the professor's words. Both Strang and Darrow dashed from the lab.

Joe waited until he heard their steps fading down the stairs. Then he burst from the curtains and rushed into the laboratory. Frank was still rigid. Joe filled a beaker with cold water from the workbench sink tap and flung it in his brother's face. Frank seemed to shudder.

"Frank! . . . Frank, can you hear me?"

Joe shook his brother and gave him several light slaps. Gradually Frank came out of the trance but appeared to have no recollection of what had happened. Joe explained hastily, adding, "Strang has the prof convinced that he's surrounded by spies—including us. An alarm just went off downstairs, and they've gone to investigate."

Frank was still a bit dazed. "I must have been blacked out by the same device used in the jewel thefts, Joe!"

"Sure, and Darrow thinks we came to steal it. We must find a way out of this place!"

"Wait a second, Joe! That alarm you mentioned

could have been Dad coming here—maybe even the police!"

"Right," Joe agreed. From the sounds he had heard, he knew there must be a front stairway. The Hardys soon found it and strained to hear what was going on below.

"Here they come now!" Strang was saying. "Looks as though they've nabbed whoever triggered the alarm!"

Frank and Joe leaned around the corner of the stair landing and peered down into the front hall. Strang was at the front door with Professor Darrow. Presently three of Strang's henchmen came in, prodding a burly prisoner at the point of a gun. Their captive had crew-cut hair and wore a gaudy checked sports jacket.

"Duke Makin!" Joe whispered in amazement.

"No sign of that kid who got away, boss," the gun-man reported. "But we caught Makin here snooping around outside."

"Good work, Barney!" Strang said approvingly.

"Barney's the man who was with Jack Wayne at Tigers' Bight!" Frank murmured in Joe's ear.

Duke Makin looked self-assured, which appeared to infuriate Strang.

"I warned you once before, Makin, to keep out of my hair!" the jewel thief rasped.

Makin laughed contemptuously. "And I told you, Strang, that I'm dealing myself in on this jewel racket of yours."

"You're not muscling in on anything, Makin, except big trouble."

Again Makin laughed. "You're the one who's got trouble. After you learned Fenton Hardy was on your case, a pal of mine in Chicago found out he was there.

I asked my pal to tip off Hardy about the Haley Building job. How did I know about it? I overheard you blokes talking after you cased Tiffman's office. And there'll be more tip-offs if I don't collect a share on every jewel haul you make from now on. I want to know what your blackout gimmick is, too."

"What's he talking about?" Professor Darrow asked Strang. "What does he mean by 'every jewel haul you make'?"

"Get back up to your lab, Professor!" Strang ordered roughly. "This man is another foreign agent—he's simply trying to pull the wool over your eyes. I'll handle him!"

Darrow obeyed meekly, but he looked bewildered as he started up the steps. Frank and Joe shrank back into the shadows. Darrow reached the top of the stairs and turned towards his laboratory without noticing them.

Meanwhile, Makin had resumed his sneering argument with Strang. "I mean business!"

"Shut up!" Strang exploded. "We know you conked Waxie at the airport and swiped those amethysts from my car—but it's the last trick you'll pull, Makin! Take him to our 'guest room,' boys. I'll attend to him later, after we find the other kid!"

They herded Makin off towards the rear of the house. Frank and Joe tiptoed cautiously down the stairs, hoping to make a break through the front door.

But suddenly Darrow called from his laboratory, "That boy we left in here—he's gone!"

With a snarl of rage, Strang came charging back into the front hall towards the stairway. Before the Hardys could retreat, he had spotted them!

· 19 ·

Jewel Cache

FRANK and Joe ran wildly up the steps, two at a time—then fled down the corridor to their right, away from the laboratory. Below, Strang had just gained the stairway and was starting up in pursuit, bellowing to his men for help.

Selecting a room at random, Joe flung open the door and the boys darted through, slamming the door behind them. Here, too, the rooms seemed to interconnect in maze-like fashion.

"Good thing Perth built such a crazy house!" Frank panted, as they darted from one room to another.

The pounding footsteps of their pursuers could be heard from various directions as if the men were spreading out. But the mansion was immense, and the boys managed to reach the back stairway and dart down to the ground floor without being seen. Joe tugged at the back door which led to a rear porch, but it refused to budge.

"They must have locked it when they were searching for us earlier—to keep us from getting out!" he muttered to Frank. The tunnel now seemed to be their best hope.

Halfway down the stairs to the basement, the boys saw Al Hirff entering through the tunnel door. With a shout, he ran towards them. Frank and Joe fled back

143

up the stairs. In the kitchen Frank grabbed up a rubbish bin and flung it towards the doorway to the main stairs. Then the brothers raced through a side hallway towards the front of the house.

Crash! They heard Hirff stumble over the rubbish bin.

A moment later an angry voice began shouting orders. It sounded like that of Strang. Steps came pounding down the front stairway, cutting off hope of escape through the front door.

"In here!" Frank urged, pausing at a room on the left. He turned the door knob and the brothers slipped inside, went through a small room, opened another door and entered a larger chamber.

In a few moments the door to the Hardys' hiding place was jerked open again. Noel Strang flicked a switched and glanced hastily around. "They must have made it out of the front door!" he exclaimed to someone in the hallway. The light went out again, the room door was shut, and footsteps hurried off.

Frank and Joe emerged from behind the heavy window curtains. They dared not switch on their torches, but gradually their eyes became accustomed to the darkness.

"It's Jerome Perth's room," Frank said. "The same one we saw from outside!"

"But now the floor feels solid," Joe murmured.

Frank was frowning as he peered about the room. "Joe, do you notice anything funny about this furniture?"

"No. What?"

"Except for that chair at the desk, every single piece of furniture in the room is placed smack up against the wall—even the armchairs."

"That *is* odd, Frank," his brother murmured. "Does that suggest something to you?"

"It sure does. It suggests that the furniture may be bolted to the wall!"

Frank tried to move an armchair, the desk, and a wardrobe. None budged!

"Well, this explains one thing," he remarked. "We know now how the furniture was able to stay suspended in mid-air when the floor wasn't there."

"Wasn't there?" Joe echoed. He was examining the way in which the headboard of the bed fitted flush to the wall. He spoke over his shoulder. "You mean you think the floor of this room really does disappear?"

As Joe turned to face Frank, his elbow rubbed against some ornamental carving in the wall panelling. The next moment both Hardys gasped.

The floor was sinking straight down under their feet!

"What did you do, Joe?" Frank exclaimed.

"Search me! My elbow just brushed the wall somewhere up there by the light switch. There must be a hidden push button or something that operates this floor!"

By this time, the whole floor had descended like an elevator to basement level, carrying the boys and the unbolted chair with it. A familiar, musty odour came suddenly to the boys' nostrils.

Frank turned on his torch and beamed it about the walls. To his right was a mouldering wooden door. This was the window side of Perth's room.

"An entrance to the tunnel!" Joe whispered.

"Did you say there's a light switch up there by the bed?" Frank inquired.

"Yes, probably a two-way switching arrangement,

so the light can be turned on or off either from the doorway or from the bed."

"Joe, I think I can explain how Perth's nephew was killed!" Frank said excitedly.

"How?"

"Remember, the nephew only lived in the mansion for a few days before his death. He probably never discovered the secret of this sinking floor."

"Wouldn't he have been curious when he saw that the furniture in his room was bolted to the walls?"

"Maybe—if he noticed. But his uncle had been a queer old chap, anyway. And evidently the servants didn't know the secret of the room, either."

"No, I suppose they didn't, if they never told about it," Joe agreed. "But I wonder how it is that they never touched the switch accidentally—say while they were cleaning the wall panelling."

Frank shrugged. "Maybe Old Man Perth told them not to clean it—or to use only a feather duster."

"Okay, I'll accept that. Go on."

"We know that Nyland's father, Karl Nyland, was snooping about the grounds the night the nephew was killed. It *could* be that he made a noise outside the windows, and the nephew heard him and woke up."

Joe nodded. "Sounds reasonable. So?"

"So the nephew gropes in the dark to turn on the light switch—and in doing so, accidentally presses the floor button, but doesn't know it."

"Wow! I get it!" Joe blurted out. "The floor starts sinking, but since the furniture is still up there, he doesn't realize what has happened!"

"Right. So he jumps out of bed, falls right down to the basement, and fractures his skull, poor fellow! Then later, when the servants came to investigate, the opening of the anteroom door raised the floor back to its normal level."

"Seems fair enough." Joe nodded. "But what if Perth had to get the floor back up from the basement? How would he do that?"

"Easy, I think. He probably had a timer set that automatically raised the basement floor if the anteroom door was out of action."

"Sure," Joe agreed. "That would be a natural feature if Perth designed this set-up as an emergency escape system—living in fear of his life as he did."

"Exactly," Frank said. "If any of his swindle victims ever forced their way into the mansion to get revenge, Perth could lower the floor to the basement and duck out through the tunnel. If the assassin actually broke into his room, he'd find it empty, the windows locked from the inside, and no trace of Old Man Perth!"

"Frank, I'll bet you've solved the mystery!" Joe said enthusiastically. "Everything fits—even the nephew's dying gasp about the floor. He was trying to tell the servants what had happened."

"The—the floor! It's going up!" Frank cried excitedly. "Into the tunnel—fast!"

The boys leaped out through the tunnel doorway and began making their way along the brick-walled passage to the summerhouse outlet. Frank was in the lead. They had gone about two-thirds of the way when he halted suddenly.

"Hold it, Joe!" Frank whispered. "Maybe this way out isn't so smart after all!"

"What do you mean?"

"Strang knows now that we got *into* the house through the tunnel."

Joe gave a low groan. "Which means there may be a guard posted near the tiled floor!"

He mulled over the possibilities. "Boy, we wouldn't have a chance to spot anybody in the dark, either. Unless we used our torches which would give *us* away!"

The boys quickly decided the risk was too great.

"I vote we try sneaking back up the basement stairs and see if we can talk Professor Darrow into helping us," Frank said.

"He was the one who gave us away in the first place," Joe objected. "And he shouted to Strang that you had escaped from the lab."

"I know, but we'd given him quite a surprise," Frank argued. "The way he looked coming up the stairs after hearing what Makin said—well, I have a hunch he's been doing a lot of thinking."

"I suppose we have no choice," Joe said. Suddenly his eyes narrowed. "Say, Frank! Take a look at that brick your light's shining on—the one that's a little darker than the others."

"What about it?"

"Looks to me as if the mortar is loose around it," Joe said tensely. "Didn't Nyland tell us that Old Man Perth boasted the partnership papers were stashed *outside* the mansion—in a place that anyone could get at?"

Frank gave his brother an excited look. "Give me your knife, Joe!"

The knife blade passed easily around all sides of the loose brick. In a moment Frank had removed it. Behind the space where the brick had been was a deep recess. It was crammed with papers and small cloth pouches!

Frank fished them out, one by one. The pouches contained a dazzling assortment of gems, cut and uncut—diamonds, emeralds, rubies, sapphires.

There were also stock certificates, bonds, and papers relating to various business deals. Among the latter was the partnership agreement between Perth and Karl Nyland, and a map of the lode site, signed with Nyland's name.

"Wow!" Joe muttered. "Do you suppose those jewels were Old Man Perth's and did Strang locate this cache, as Karl Nyland Jr thinks?"

"Nyland's right. Strang found it and he's also using the tunnel as a place to hide his loot till the heat's off. One of those bags of diamonds is labelled for delivery to Paul Tiffman."

"This would also explain about Karl Nyland's amethysts—the ones his father brought to Perth," Joe reasoned. "Strang found them here and decided to peddle them, since they weren't 'hot.' But Makin stole them from the glove compartment of Strang's car."

The boys crammed their pockets with part of the loot, and stuffed the rest inside their shirts. They also took the partnership papers. Then they headed back through the tunnel to the basement.

The house was quiet. Frank and Joe wondered if the men were searching the grounds. The boys tiptoed up the back stairway to the top floor, then made their way down the corridor to the laboratory.

Professor Darrow was seated at his workbench, holding his head in his hands. He looked up with a start as the boys entered. His face was drawn and pale. To the Hardys' relief, he showed no sign of hostility, and made no effort to call for help.

"Are you really Fenton Hardy's sons?" he asked, then brushed aside the boys' attempt to show him identification from their wallets. "Never mind—papers of any kind can be forged. The important thing is, I believe now that *you* and not Strang are telling me the truth."

"I suppose what Duke Makin said convinced you," Frank said quietly.

Darrow nodded listlessly. "I've been a terrible fool. Strang led me to believe that he would finance my work for the public good. Instead, he was only interested in using my paralysing-ray device to commit crimes."

"If you need any other proof," Frank said, "we found where he had hidden the loot from his jewel thefts, and we have it all right here."

"The main thing now," Joe said, "is to call Dad and the police. Can I use that phone over there?"

Again Darrow nodded. "Do so, by all means."

Joe lifted the telephone from its cradle and started to dial. Suddenly a cold, menacing laugh came over the receiver and the line went dead!

·20·

Trapped!

Joe hung up with a gasp of dismay and turned to Frank. "Someone just broke in and cut me off!" he exclaimed. "It sounded like Strang!"

"Would Strang know what room the call was coming from?" Frank asked the professor.

Darrow looked at the boys unhappily. "Yes. My phone line evidently is tapped—perhaps a signal device warns Strang when I lift the receiver. Sometimes when I'd attempt to make an outside call, he would cut me off. His excuse was that he was keeping me safe from detection by foreign spies."

"Come on!" Joe broke in. "Run for it!"

Darrow made no effort to escape, but the Hardys darted down the corridor towards the back stairs. Strang, Barney, and another henchman already were on their way up. Frank and Joe fled towards the front of the mansion, only to find Hirff and two others dashing up the front stairs.

"Into the lab!" Frank urged. "We'll try the window —maybe we can slide down the drainpipe!"

The boys hastily retreated to the laboratory. They were just flinging up the window sash when the criminals burst through the door and aimed two small, portable ray guns at them.

"Hold it or we'll freeze you stiffer than iced mackerels!" Strang shouted as the boys turned to confront their captors. "These little rods we're holding are miniature models of that fancy gadget the prof used on you before. We've found them extremely handy on jewel thefts."

"Please!" Darrow protested weakly. "These boys have done you no harm. Let them go. Perhaps they'll agree not to turn you in."

"Shut up, you sap!" Strang's voice cracked like a whiplash. "You're in this as deep as any of us! Do you think we can let these kids go now, knowing all about our racket?"

Darrow shrank back as Strang proceeded to jeer at him.

"I conned you from the start, you egghead! Did you really think I'd sink good money into this set-up just so you could develop these blackout guns for national defence? And you swallowed all that junk about spies.

"What you were really doing here, Darrow, was getting us ready for the biggest jewel-theft operation in history. Those purple tear-gas grenades you cooked up were an extra bonus!"

Strang's henchmen roared with laughter. Their response spurred him to greater boasting and he answered Frank's and Joe's questions freely. The first hint that the Hardys might be on his trail had come when the boys had followed him in his car.

The ghostly screams had warned the gang that someone was prowling near their tunnel exit, so next morning they had camouflaged the tiled floor with turf and brush. In doing so, they had found the knife bearing Frank's name. Then later, one of the men had used the exit and had left the tiles uncovered. When Strang had found Frank's knife, he thought the Hardys had seen the floor.

Knowing from newspaper accounts of their earlier cases that the boys owned a boat, Strang had ordered two of his men to sabotage it. "I saw then it was time to scare you pests off or get rid of you for good," Strang went on. The brothers had escaped with their lives— but later, when the *Napoli* had happened to anchor near the *Seacat*, one of the gang, known as Moose, had attacked Joe in the bay.

As the Hardys had suspected, Strang had sent two of his men, Kelso and Trigger, to Chicago to pull the Spyker robbery, after telephoning a false clue to Mr Hardy.

Strang had arranged to be aboard the chartered plane at the time of the robbery, in order to establish an alibi in case he was charged with the theft. He had arrived in Chicago in time to organize the transfer of the loot, stowing it in a secret compartment of Hirff's plane and later taking it to the Perth mansion hideout.

Kelso and Trigger had gone to Gary, Indiana, to plant the decoy getaway car, then returned to Bayport by commercial airliner.

"How did Makin happen to be at the airport the night of the robbery?" Frank asked.

"He trailed Waxie, who was waiting for me to fly in from Chicago. But he didn't wait long before Makin jumped him, and made him unlock Hirff's hangar so he could search it.

"Then he took Waxie back to the car and found the amethysts in the glove compartment. He knocked Waxie out and was going to leave him there, unconscious, as a warning that we should cut him in. But when you kids and that private eye showed up and spotted him, Makin took off. And when I came in, I had to leave the loot in Hirff's plane and take a taxi back to the mansion."

The gang had rented the cabin at Tigers' Bight as an emergency hideout, intending to flee there in their cruiser if the police should close in. Jack Wayne had been taken there by Barney after he had contacted the *Seacat* by radio.

"What were you planning to do with Jack?" Joe asked.

"He told Hirff your dad owed him money and wouldn't pay up—so now he was sore at you Hardys and looking for some quick dough. We thought if he was telling the truth, he might tell us how much you knew. If not, we'd get rid of him fast. Barney was keeping him at the cabin till I got a chance to question him."

After Joe had photographed the chart found in Hirff's plane, Hirff had phoned the news to Strang, and the gang had tried to snatch the film. When that move failed, Strang had radioed Barney to booby-trap the cabin and take off in *Skyhappy Sal* before the Hardys could get there.

On the Haley Building job, Kelso had learned about the delivery from a stooge in the jewellery company. Kelso had entered the building during business hours and had hidden in a washroom. Later, he had let Waxie in by the fire-escape door.

The two had sneaked downstairs to the entrance hall, where the watchman had been seated at his desk with his back to the stairway. They had blasted him with the ray gun.

Kelso then had tampered with the lift and Waxie had installed duplicate fifth-floor numbers and name plates on the sixth-floor offices. Kelso had posed as Paul Tiffman to receive the diamonds from the messenger. The robbery accomplished, they had again blacked out the watchman and removed all traces of their ruse.

"How did Makin learn you were planning to pull the job?" Frank asked.

Strang chuckled. "We squeezed that out of him before we blacked him out. He was watching the mansion that day and trailed Kelso to the building. When Kelso never came out, he figured we were planning to pull a job there."

"How about that voice I heard over your tunnel intercom?" Joe put in, to keep Strang talking.

The jewel thief laughed. "Pretty fast thinking on your part, kid—I'll hand you that much. Trigger thought Waxie had forgotten his orders and was calling for a quick fill-in."

"Good thing I realized the person on the line wasn't Waxie," Trigger said. "He's a nut! Crazy about the gadgets in this place. Calling on the intercom. Pushing the floor release in that rigged-up room."

"Maybe Waxie forgot to put the floor back in place the night we first saw it through the window," Frank suggested, still playing for time.

"Waxie forgot once too often," Strang grunted. "Last time, I nearly broke a leg. Got fed up. Lucky for Waxie he scrammed when he did."

Meanwhile, Professor Darrow had furtively plugged

in his blackout invention. Suddenly he snatched it up and aimed the machine at the thieves. But Trigger saw the manoeuvre.

"Look out, boss!" the gangster yelled, whipping out his own ray gun to fire.

Strang jumped clear in the nick of time. But Trigger had no chance to use his own gun. The blaze of brilliance from the professor's machine paralysed all five of Strang's henchmen.

Strang's own leap had left him momentarily off balance. The Hardys seized their chance. Frank stunned the gang boss with a hard right to the jaw. Joe wrestled away his blackout gun, and in a few moments the two young sleuths had punched Strang into submission.

"It would be safer if I blacked him out," Professor Darrow suggested to the boys. "The rays from my device do no permanent damage. They simply effect certain brain centres and temporarily immobilize the subject until the neural circuits have time to clear themselves."

"Maybe he has a point there," Joe remarked to Frank with a grin. "We have no handcuffs."

As the professor was blacking out Strang, Frank spotted car headlights through the trees surrounding the mansion. A short time later Fenton Hardy, Chief Collig, and a squad of police rushed into the house to take over. They stared in amazement when they saw the helpless members of the gang.

"Looks as though we missed the preliminaries *and* the main event," the tall investigator remarked to Collig with a chuckle. "They're all out cold."

The chief and his men grinned in satisfaction. "I'd

say six KO's are enough of a show for any evening!"
Collig quipped.

"Seven." Joe grinned. "I think you'll find another
KO in the 'guest room.' "

After hearing the whole story, Mr Hardy and the
chief were warm in their praise of Frank and Joe. But
the boys pointed out that it was Professor Darrow who
had brought victory at the last moment.

"I'm afraid you've been badly misled, Professor,"
Mr Hardy said. "Some facts you may not know are
these: Strang and his men had their eye on the Perth
mansion as a hideout. When you bought it, they
arranged to move in with you and used the ray gun as
an excuse."

Frank added, "And Makin, in trying to worm his
way into the gang, offered to rent the place. He only
wanted to find out if Strang's group were just helping
themselves to the mansion."

Mr Hardy went on, "But, Professor, you certainly
turned the tables on the gang! I'm reasonably sure
that any charges against you, for your part in Strang's
operation, will be dropped."

"How did you happen to get here, Dad?" Frank
asked as the police were removing the prisoners.

"After I heard Tony and Chet's story, and you two
failed to return, I decided it was time to blow the
whistle on this set-up at the mansion," Fenton Hardy
replied, throwing an arm around each of his boys.

"What I'd like to know is who rigged all those spooky
alarm devices," Joe spoke up.

Professor Darrow gave a wan smile. "I did, partly
to keep off intruders and partly for my own amusement,"
he explained. "It was while I was wiring them into

the mansion's electrical system that I stumbled on the bedroom-study's disappearing floor and told Strang about it."

Next day the stolen rented motorboat was located, and the Hardys went to the hospital to see Jack Wayne, who had regained consciousness and was rapidly recovering.

"So you've wrapped up the case, eh?" the pilot said.

"Frank and Joe have," Mr Hardy answered. "But we all feel bad about the loss of *Skyhappy Sal*."

Jack grinned. "Don't worry. She was insured, so I'll have a new *Sal* pretty soon."

"Dad says there'll be a good bit of reward money," Frank put in, "and you'll get half, Jack. That should buy your new *Sal* a lot of fancy trimmings."

"We're still curious about that interrupted radio message of yours, Jack," said Joe. "How about spelling the whole message out for us?"

Jack thought for a moment, then asked for pencil and paper and wrote down the message as nearly as he could remember it. The boys bracketed the words which had been lost in transmission. The result read:

[I'M FLYING DOWN TO TIGERS' BIGHT TO SEE A FELLOW HIRFF TOLD ME ABOUT. HE SAYS THAT] IF THE TIGERS' BIGHT [SET-UP CAN USE A PILOT, I COULD MAKE A LOT OF CASH. I'M TO USE THE CODE NAME] AMETHYST [TO IDENTIFY MYSELF].

A few days later the stones Makin had stolen were recovered, and an expert survey of the amethyst location showed that the lode, while not highly valuable as a source of ornamental gems, was worth developing for commercial purposes. The story was repeated at the Morton farm to Tony and Chet.

"That's a break for Nyland," Frank commented. "Joe and I had decided to use part of our share of the reward money to pay his wife's hospital bills—but now—"

"My share's going to help my folks buy a new car," said Tony.

"You guys have no imagination," Chet retorted.

"Listen, Chet, how about using your part to buy some detective equipment so you can help Frank and me on our next case?" Joe teased, not knowing that very soon they would indeed be called on to solve the *Mystery of the Desert Giant.*

"Oh yes?" Chet retorted. "Hop over to the Bayport Soda Shop with me, and I'll show you what *I'm* investing in—a year's supply of the biggest banana splits you ever saw!"

has a whole shipload of exciting books for you

Armadas are chosen by children all over the world. They're designed to fit your pocket, and your pocket money too. They're colourful, exciting, and there are hundreds of titles to choose from. Armada has something for everyone:

Mystery and adventure series to collect, with favourite characters and authors . . . like Alfred Hitchcock and The Three Investigators – The Hardy Boys – young detective Nancy Drew – the intrepid Lone Piners – Biggles – the rascally William – and others.

Hair-raising Spinechillers – Ghost, Monster and Science Fiction stories. Fascinating quiz and puzzle books. Exciting hobby books. Lots of hilarious fun books. Many famous stories. Thrilling pony adventures. Popular school stories – and many more.

You can build up your own Armada collection – and new Armadas are published every month, so look out for the latest additions to the Captain's cargo.

Armadas are available in bookshops and newsagents.

Armada